The Highbinders

By F. M. Parker

SHADOW OF THE WOLF
THE SEARCHER
COLDIRON
NIGHTHAWK
SKINNER

The Highbinders

F. M. PARKER

DOUBLEDAY & COMPANY, INC.

GARDEN CITY, NEW YORK

1986

Library of Congress Cataloging-in-Publication Data

Parker, F. M.
The highbinders.

I. Title.
PS3566.A678H5   1986   813'.54   85-29250
ISBN 0-385-23587-9

The Highbinders

The Golden Cube—A Prologue

Over aeons of time, the hot, primeval earth cooled and powerful convection currents, reaching to the very core of the molten sphere, lifted up the lighter elements and concentrated them upon the surface like a thin froth. Vast quantities of heat continued to radiate away into space during additional millions of years. The froth hardened into one giant land mass.

Mighty forces broke the land mass into segments and slid them chip-like upon the denser interior of the planet. These continents arched and buckled under the thrusting force, creating tall mountain ranges upon their backs. From the hot center of the planet, mineral-rich fluids and gases were pumped into the passageways of the fractures and ruptures.

Upon one such land mass there was a mountain that received part of these deep earth fluids. As the emanations migrated upward away from their source, they found regions that were cooler and had less pressure. The minerals that could not remain in solution in the new environs differentiated and precipitated out in the cracks and fissures of the mountain. Remaining behind to continue the journey through the rocks was a mixture becoming ever more concentrated with the more volatile and mobile of the compounds.

In a place far underground within the mountain was a cavity, a very insignificant void as measured on the scale of the mountain. The percolating fluids containing the final elements entered the cavity. The temperature and pressure that existed there breached the fine line of mobility of one element.

One atom of this metal settled from the liquid to rest upon the bottom of the void. A second atom attached itself to the first. And then a third joined its brothers.

Preordained by the order of the universe, the atoms could join with each other in only one physical structure. As millions, billions of additional atoms dropped from solution, they formed themselves into a crystal lattice, aligning themselves with infinite precision, straight lines, right angles—a perfect cube.

Time passed, an unimaginable span, and more billions of the particles of the mineral added their mass to the cube. Its edges were always sharp, sharp to the dimensions of one atom.

Finally the passageways through the rocks closed and the mineral-laden fluids ceased to flow. Left resting in the cavity of the mountain was a perfect metal cube, three inches on each side by human measurement.

Over uncounted epochs of time, wind and water eroded the mountain and earthquakes jarred down mammoth slabs and blocks of its flanks. One day the last weathered fragment of the rock that had been the host of the cube fell away. The sun shone upon the cube for the very first time, a glorious yellow nugget of gold.

The magnificent golden nugget tumbled from its resting place and over the ensuing millenniums rolled and slid down the bottom of a steep creek to a mighty river.

The cube was swept by the river onto a gravel bar. Floods buried it.

The cube once again lay hidden from the sun.

CHAPTER 1

Honeycomb Badlands, Oregon—November 6, 1869

The body of the outlaw lay wrapped in the blue Indian blanket beside the half-dug grave. In the bottom of the excavation, Sheriff Gumert dug with a short-handled shovel, the iron blade ringing harshly with each blow upon the stony earth of the badlands.

Gumert stopped his labor, and lifting his hat, flicked beads of sweat from his forehead with a calloused finger. He looked out across the inhospitable and nearly impassable rock hill and sharp rock pinnacles forming the cells of the imaginary honeycombs.

The barren land stretched away mile upon weary mile in every direction. It had been formed by the erosion of a great blanket of volcanic debris that had in some long-ago time exploded with fiery violence onto the land. Wind and water had carved and sculptured the ash and rock into a steep, angular topography hundreds of feet tall.

The moisture of rain and snow had dissolved the crystals of iron in the tuff to stain the tortured rock mass with splotches of deep reds and browns. Like an army of men had dripped its lifeblood on the Honeycombs.

Access into the jagged and broken terrain was possible only along the gravelly beds of the dry washes. Squeezed in between the more welded and enduring knobs of tuff, the gullies twisted and curved in strange and unpredictable paths. It was a land without pattern, easy for a man to wander lost in its labyrinthine channels.

Thunder rumbled, sweeping north across the badlands from the distant Alvord Desert. All afternoon, clouds had been building in the heated updrafts rising above the dusty, flour-white surface of the desert. The boiling masses of moisture, towering nine, ten miles high above the ancient dry lake bed, hung nervously electric, seething with energy. Some of the thunderheads had grown powerful enough to exist without the desert, and were striding like giants up from the Alvord into the southern edge of the Honeycombs.

Brilliant bolts of lightning flashed down from the dark bottoms of the storm clouds to slam the earth. Thunder crashed menacingly, like the pounding of huge cannons. Rain began to fall in long slanting streamers from the swollen stomachs of the clouds.

Swift wind swept out more than a score of miles ahead of the storm front to dart among the cinder cones and rock pinnacles. The wind, carrying a chill down from the frigid zones of the high atmosphere where it had been born, swirled up the dust to fling it in a billowing surf through the dry gullies.

A strong gust of the grit-laden air buffeted the sheriff and flopped the wide brim of his hat. He turned and looked to investigate the condition of one of his deputies lying unconscious in the shade of a ledge of rock.

Basker was bruised in many places, his left leg was broken a few inches below the knee. The leg had been bound in a folded blanket and then tied rigidly between two rifles to prevent the bones from moving and worsening the wound.

Garrity, his second deputy, was riding toward the Owyhee River lying a dozen miles to the west. The fast-flowing river, fed by snow melt from the faraway Santa Rosa and Tuscarora mountains of Nevada and the closer Owyhee Mountains on the border between Idaho and Oregon, forced its wet course through the desert and skirted the west boundary of the badlands. Cottonwood trees grew on the bank of the river. Garrity should return soon with long poles from one of those stands of trees to make a horse-drawn travois to transport the injured Basker to a doctor in Westfall.

Two saddle horses and a pack animal had been ground-tied down the slope of the land from the grave. The black horse that had once belonged to the outlaw had dragged its reins and drawn near the body of its master. His pointed ears were thrust at the body in an intent, listening attitude. He sniffed at the blanket. Catching hold of a loose fold with his teeth, he tugged at it and nickered plaintively.

At the sound, the sheriff turned about to look at the horse. It was an excellent animal, with long legs and deep chest. However, he was getting old with a wide band of gray around the muzzle and gray hairs here and there in the black coat of the still muscular body. The horse must be as old as the dead outlaw.

The horse nudged the shoulder of the blanketed form as if trying to waken the man. The action bothered the sheriff. He picked up a rock and threw it, striking the animal on the side. The startled beast pivoted away for a few steps. Then he came hesitantly, warily back, watching the sheriff with alert black eyes, to stand over the motionless body again.

The dark shadow of a cloud slid silently in to dim the land. The sheriff examined the swiftly traveling thunderheads. Rain would be falling in a few minutes and a torrent flooding through the arroyos. He wanted the grave to be finished before that happened. He glanced at the blanket-shrouded figure, measuring it against the length and width of the hole. Then he lowered his head and began to dig hurriedly.

A voice called out behind the sheriff. "Gumert, what is going on?"

The sheriff turned his head to find Basker had regained consciousness and dragged himself from under the rock cliff.

The deputy thrust a hand at the black horse and then down at the figure of the man. "Where did that animal come from and who's that in the blanket?"

"That's Tom Gallatin's horse and that's Gallatin's body."

Basker groaned. "Goddamn no. It can't be. What happened to him?"

"What do you mean? You can see he's dead. I killed him with my Sharps 56. Damn fine shot too. Nearly a quarter-mile range and I got him through the head."

An expression of dismay swept over the deputy's face. The look quickly changed to anger. "You're a sonofabitch, Gumert. You always have been too ready to use that big gun. I owed that man my life."

Gumert spread his legs and planted his feet firmly in the bottom of the grave. "Stop yelling at me, Basker, and tell me why you think you owe this man anything."

Basker glared at the sheriff. "He saved my life, that's what. It happened after we split up near the lava field to find his trail again. You went west and Garrity east to circle outside the lava where there was soil to mark a horse's tracks. I went straight on across the lava like you told me to." Basker stopped talking and looked at the body for a moment.

He shook his head sadly and began to speak again. "My fool horse stepped in a crack in the lava and fell. Landed on my leg and broke it. Twisted his own hoof most off with the bone showing. I shot the clumsy thing.

"I started hauling myself across that lava rock. Damnation, it was sharp as glass and I was soon cut and bleeding. After a time I stopped to rest. Didn't seem like I had made any headways at all. There was miles yet to go. I thought right then, that I might die out there. With all the ridges and hollows and slabs of lava standing on end, you and Garrity might never find me.

"I started to crawl again. Then I heard this noise on the rocks near me." Basker pointed at the black animal. "That big horse there was standing beside me. And a fellow was glaring down at me, cold as ice. I knew it was Gallatin right off. It had to be him way out in that godforsaken lava country."

The sheriff climbed out of the grave and came to kneel close to Basker. "What did he look like? When I got to see him after he was shot, there was blood all covering his face."

"A young man, hardly more than a grown boy. Black hair. Tall, but skinny, like he hadn't eaten right for some time."

Gumert nodded. "Yeh. I saw he was bony-looking when I rolled him in the blanket."

Basker spoke. "Gallatin steps down from his horse and squats close to me. I figured it wasn't any accident he was there. Probably heard my pistol shot when I killed my horse. He had a six-gun on his hip and I figured since we had been hounding his trail for better than five days, well he was going to be damn mad and would shoot me sure as hell.

"Quick as thought, he snatches my pistol from its holster. Then he stands up and watches out over the lava for a long time. I suspected he was looking for the rest of the posse, you and Garrity, to see how close you might be before he killed me.

"But that's not what he did."

Basker pointed at a large tear in the front of his shirt. "That's where I had my badge fastened. Well, Gallatin just reached out and grabs that piece of tin and tore it off. He throws it way out on the lava rock.

"Then he talks to me in a voice soft as a preacher. 'You're not a lawman anymore. You're just a man with a broke leg that needs help. Where can I take you so your friends can find you?'

"Well, I think it is all some kind of mean trick he is playing. But I tell him that you will be expecting to meet me at the north end of the lava field. And what does he do? Well, he lifts me up, strong he was and gentle, and sets me in his own saddle. Him leading that horse, off we go. I swear that old horse is as nimble-footed as a goat, for he never made one false step.

"Damn it, Gumert, he spent five or six hours packing me out. If he hadn't done that, he could've been miles gone from us and safe somewhere far away."

"Yes, he could have been," agreed the sheriff. "John Manderfield told me Gallatin was an odd fellow.

"He came in off the Alvord Desert in a sandstorm one day. He stopped at the first place where there were people. That was the Manderfield ranch. He stayed there a few days. Manderfield said he never spoke one word as to who he was. He asked a lot of questions about everything and always listened right close to the answers.

"He had long hair tied back with rawhide. His clothes were hand-me-down and all badly worn and patched. He wore a six-gun. The old rancher was the only person who ever talked with Gallatin. Except for the Fettus brothers."

"Yeh. The damn Fettus brothers," growled Basker. "They were always roughhousing someone or playing some tomfool prank. This time they ran up against the wrong fellow who did not want to play their game and it turned into real trouble."

"Manderfield saw the whole thing," said Gumert. "Gallatin went to Westfall to get a haircut and some new clothes. The Fettuses blocked his way so he couldn't go along the sidewalk to the barbershop. Gallatin went out into the street to go around them. They moved again to stop him. They poked fun at him and called him names. Manderfield said Gallatin seemed confused as to what to do about it all. Then Buck Fettus made the mistake of touching his six-gun. From that moment on, Gallatin knew what to do. He drew his pistol and killed Buck, and just kept on triggering his gun, killing Ollie and Oscar. One shot was all that was needed for each of them.

"That's where Gallatin went wrong. If he had killed only Buck, then that could've been called self-defense. But he shot the other two brothers, too. Neither of them had reached for their guns."

"Maybe they didn't have time," said Basker.

"Maybe so," responded Gumert. "Manderfield said Gallatin made the fastest, smoothest draw he had ever seen. All three Fettuses were dead in the dirt in a fraction of a second. Someone really trained that young man first-rate.

"Gallatin should've stuck around for a trial. But instead, he climbs up on that big horse and rides away. It was my sworn duty as sheriff to go after him to bring him back."

"We weren't anyplace close to catching Gallatin until he stopped to help me. He seemed to know the location of every water hole and all the paths through the mountains and badlands. Then you used that long-distance killing gun on him without giving him a chance. Gumert, you did wrong."

"Basker, you listen to me good," snapped Gumert. "Garrity and me looked for you at the rendezvous point. You were no place around. We go off trying to find you. When I get back, there you were looking like death on the ground. Tom Gallatin was galloping off. I thought he had killed you like he did the Fettuses. So I jerked out my Sharps and shot. I know now it was a mistake. But right then it seemed the right thing to do. Damn it, man, don't you understand? I thought he had killed one of my deputies."

Basker did not reply. He saw the strain on the sheriff's face at the unexpected turn of events.

Gumert looked away and out over the angular rock structures of the badlands. Three men were dead because they had tried their bullying hassle on a young man who thought the game was for life or death. Then the sheriff himself misinterpreted what he saw and killed a fourth man. All dead for nothing. Damn sad happenings.

The first big raindrops of the storm began to drum on the ground and splatter on the rocks. Gumert evaluated the thunderhead charging upon them and then turned to Basker. "This is going to be a mighty cold rain. Let me help you back under the rock ledge. I think I'll climb in there with you for there's enough room."

Both men peered out through the thickening rain. The body of the outlaw could barely be seen beside the grave.

Basker spoke. "I wish we had got him buried before the storm hit. It doesn't seem right for him to be laying there in the wet like that."

"Dead men don't feel anything," responded the sheriff.

The sky darkened as if night were falling. The air split open and rain poured in a deluge, drenching the badlands. Water collected in every crevice, gathered into streams and poured into the gullies.

The black horse shifted his rump toward the wind and humped his back against the wet onslaught, but he did not move from beside his master.

The cold deepened and the intensity of the rain increased as the core of the storm arrived. The frigid moisture swiftly soaked the wool blanket encasing the body of Tom Gallatin. Icy rivulets washed over his bloody face and saturated his clothing. He became immersed in a chilling bath.

The battered brain within the bullet-damaged skull sensed the sudden shock of the cold. It drew back from where it hovered on the shadowy border beyond which was death.

With the awakening of the brain, Tom felt the pain. Oh God! The pain! His skull was broken open and someone was pouring molten lead into it. The outlaw's body trembled with the intensity of the agony. His ams and legs jerked spasmodically against the blanket.

Tom Gallatin became conscious lying in a black arctic winter. What was happening? Why was it happening to him?

A terrifying thought—Was he dying?

The mind reached out through the pain to test the remainder of the body and found the heart flickering erratically. And the lungs moving feebly, almost undetectably, on the verge of ceasing to beat.

The brain struggled to override the damage done by the grievous wound. It ordered the body to live.

The heart gathered strength and the blood warmed and increased its sluggish pace through the arteries. The lungs arched and sucked at the damp air.

Something was wound tightly about his body holding him imprisoned. Tom tried to force the obstacle away. The effort almost snuffed out the light of his awakening as the pain soared upward, screeching to a crescendo, searing every nerve ending.

Tom held himself still. As the body quieted, the agony lessened to merely torture. Slowly he felt of the thing that trapped him.

His hand found an opening and extended out into the driving rain. He pulled the edges of the blanket apart, exposing himself from the waist up to the storm.

The strike of the falling raindrops was hammer blows upon his maimed head. His hands rose to try and hold them off. He sat up weakly, bracing himself against the muddy ground.

All about lay a murky darkness. Thunder shook the earth. Everything—even those close—was indistinct, distorted. Some large object was standing on his right.

He worked his feet free and rolled slowly to his knees. The movement caused his gorge to rise and he heaved, trying to vomit. The muscles surrounding his empty stomach contracted, trying desperately to void the cavity. He strained with one dry heave after another. The anguish in his head surged. Maybe it was better to die.

He laughed like a madman at the thought. He was already dead and this was hell. But then this was too awful even for hell.

Something touched the side of his face and he thrust out a hand defensively. The hairy muzzle of a horse met his outstretched fingers.

Tom peered questioningly at the animal. "Sorry, old fellow, there's something wrong with my eyes. Come a little closer so I can see you better. Do I know you?"

The horse nickered and lowered his head to nuzzle the side of the young man's face.

Tom began to shiver with the cold and drew the blanket up over his head and shoulders. The sodden covering partially shielded him from the rain.

An urgent thought, colder than the storm, ran along his spine. He knew he should not be sitting there, but rather riding swiftly away. Which direction should he go? Where to? Would the horse know?

Tom struggled to his feet. He gathered up the reins and leaned limply on the horse. He would never be able to climb up on the tall back. Somehow the thought of having a horse he could not mount was crazily funny and he began to laugh wildly into the growing din of the storm.

He ceased his laughter to lick at the rainwater cascading down his face and wet his dry throat. He stripped off the soaked blanket and laid it across the horse's neck. His hands found the saddle horn and his foot went into the stirrup, and he hung there, unable to complete the task.

The insistent clamor of warning that he must escape this place charged his body with a feeble strength. He fought the sodden weight of his body up into the saddle.

"Go. You know the way," Tom ordered the horse.

The mount raised his head, listening for a more definite order or the touch of the reins that would tell him what to do. The man waited for the animal to move out.

"Go," Tom ordered the horse and pressed his heels in its ribs. "Go in any direction. We cannot stay here."

The faithful mount stepped forward, going north along a winding stream channel rapidly filling with a speeding, muddy maelstrom. With each hoof fall of the animal, the outlaw groaned as the sickening pain beat against the walls of his skull.

CHAPTER 2

The thunderstorm rumbled its way off the badlands to the northeast. The torrential rain slackened and the trailing winds whisked away. The muddy rush of water in the arroyos began to slacken their wild flows.

The sheriff peered out from the cliff into the Honeycombs, made dark and dismal by the wetness. "The storm is heading for the Snake River country."

"Gumert, look! Gallatin's body is gone," cried Basker.

"I'll be damned!" exclaimed Gumert.

"The ground is sloping toward the grave. Do you suppose the water could have washed him in?"

"Hardly likely," grunted Gumert.

"The black horse is gone, too. Are you sure he was dead?"

"He was dead. I couldn't feel any heartbeat or breath. Plenty peculiar. I'll go take a look."

"Help me, Gumert. I want to go down there with you."

"You shouldn't use that broke leg at all."

"Just help me and let me worry about the leg."

"All right. Lean on me as much as you need to."

Gumert crawled from beneath the rock ledge and lifted Basker up. With the sheriff supporting most of the injured man's weight, the two waded the sloppy mud, and drew near the excavation.

"The grave's full of dirty water," said Basker.

Gumert scanned the land beyond the water-filled hole. His gray horse and the pack animal stood nearby, wet coats plastered to their bodies and still dribbling drops of water from the long hairs on their bellies. There was no sign on the ground that the black horse or the outlaw had ever existed.

The sheriff ranged his sight over the rocky hills and flooding arroyos. Gallatin, I thought you were dead, but it appears you were not. Somewhere out there in a piece of the meanest country in the whole godforsaken world and with your head cracked open by my big rifle bullet, you are trying to escape. I wouldn't wager a grain of sand for your chances of survival.

Gumert mulled his knowledge of the badlands. A man could go north and by crossing two low divides from one watershed to another, reach the junction of the Owyhee River with the larger Snake River. That was a distance of twenty miles or better. A straighter, shorter course to get out of the badlands was to go west. Garrity should be somewhere on that route and had a good opportunity to recapture Gallatin. The lava flow lay south and east. No man and horse could navigate that tumble of rocks and crevices in such a storm as had just occurred.

Gallatin, I think you are going to die. However, you did help Basker. For that, I will give you your chance at leaving this place.

"Basker, let me set you down there on the ground so I can use the shovel. I want to bury Gallatin."

"You think he's in the grave under that water?"

"I know he's in there," said Gumert as he lowered Basker down. He looked directly into the deputy's eyes. "Don't you know it, too?"

Basker stared steadily back and replied in a strong voice. "I'm positive about him being in the grave. Fill it up and tamp down the dirt."

The black horse carried its injured rider late into the night. Beneath a moonless sky, the desert stars hung bright and hard and close to the earth. As the constellations wheeled westerly, the warmth of the day leaked away and a crisp cold settled upon the badlands.

Near midnight the horse left the muddy path of the storm and came down from the gloomy hills of the Honeycombs. The tired animal halted at the narrow point of land where the swift current of the Owyhee River rushed out from its deep canyon at the base of Freezeout Mountain and joined the slower flow of the broad Snake River.

Tom climbed weakly down from the back of the horse. He moved tenderly to prevent jarring his maimed head and sharpening the intensity of the pain.

He pulled the blanket from off the horse's neck, and shivering with the cold, wrapped the wool covering about himself and sank down to the sandy riverbank.

For a few seconds, Tom held his pain and weariness at bay as he recalled past events. He had brought the injured lawman off the lava and left him where his comrades could find him. Then something had struck him, knocking him from the saddle, to send him tumbling and cartwheeling over the ground. Complete blackness had caught him like a thunderclap.

He gingerly touched his sore head. A bullet wound, he guessed. He should not have turned aside to help the deputy, but the deed was done. Now he must escape the lawmen that pursued him.

Tom's grip on the world slipped away from him. The blackness of the night pushed into his broken skull. Partially unconscious and partially asleep, he lay beside the waters of the two rivers.

The cayuse pointed his ears here and there and his eyes roamed about to examine the spit of land and the flows of the water lapping close on both sides. He heard the noise of the muted struggle as the powerful Snake River conquered the vigorous Owyhee.

The wet sounds stirred the cayuse. Stepping carefully so not to harm the man lying at his feet, the horse went to the edge of the water and slaked his thirst.

The animal turned his attention to the sedges and grass growing on the damp bank. His hunger was deep and he began to crop the tasty reeds with his big teeth.

The horse had grazed only a short way along the river when he caught the musky scent of mountain lion. He lifted his head and sucked in a slow breath, testing, measuring the nearness of his ancient enemy. His ears reached out for sound.

The odor was diffused after drifting from the rock cliffs on the far side of the Owyhee. Even as the horse decided the swift current separated him from the big cat, the scent passed on with the breeze and could not be further detected.

For several minutes, the wary mustang searched with his night-seeing eyes into the darkness lying dense on the river. Nothing stirred except the undulation of the water. The only odor was the smell of fresh water, and the wet sand, and the tantalizing grass.

The horse grazed for a time and then returned to the man. The animal splayed his legs and rested while standing sentinel over his master.

Pearl River Valley, Kwangtung Province, China—November 6, 1869

Pak Ho, warrior captain in the Hung Society, completed his inspection of the palatial residence of Wu Ping Chin, a man who had become very rich as a merchant and now carried the title of Howqua. Pak's eight warrior guards were awake and alert and all the family of the great Howqua were safe. Pak directed his steps down the slope of the hill toward the giant warehouses on the riverbank.

He was tall for a Chinaman. His head was shaven bare for a full three inches in front and a long braid of hair, a queue, hung to his waist in the back. He, like all of the other men of the nation, wore their hair in this fashion, the fashion of the ruling Manchus, to show loyalty to these new conquerors.

Pak moved soft-footed through the blackness of the night. He avoided the lantern-lit carriage lane and went along a steep, twisting footpath. He halted on the flat ground at the end of the first warehouse and listened into the darkness.

There was no sound among the large wooden buildings or from the river beyond. Overhead, dense clouds skidded fast through the heavens, racing on the sky wind, while on the land no breeze stirred. Somehow that peculiar divergence of movement between the sky and the earth cast a feeling of discord over Pak. Was it an ill omen? Did it portend conflict to come? His strong hand felt the handle of the sharp sword on his side.

With noiseless steps, Pak went beside one of the long warehouses and crossed the pier jutting out over the water. He stopped and stood silently near a thick post used for mooring the freighter junks.

The pier was made of large pilings sunk deeply in the mud and sand of the river bottom and decked with wooden planks. The structure extended for two hundred yards along the bank of the river.

During the daylight hours, a score of junks tied up beside the wharf. Their holds and decks would be laden with goods of a hundred varieties, ferried upriver from Lintin Island where the deep-drafted, ocean-going ships were required to anchor. Sweating laborers quickly unloaded the vessels. Then, reloaded with outbound cargo and sails full of wind, the junks raced away with the current.

At Pak's feet, the mighty Pearl River slid past in the night. He knew well its course that continued southeast to pass the city of Whampoa, then onward between Hong Kong and Macao, finally to empty its prodigious flow of water into the salty brine of the South China Sea.

The oily surface of the river reflected a star as the cloud layer parted to expose a sliver of sky. As the surroundings brightened slightly, Pak turned and surveyed the hulking bulks of the three cavernous warehouses spaced along the wharf and extending back to the base of the hill. The buildings contained many fortunes of jade, tea, fur, silk, sandalwood, metal ores and a hundred other items stored and awaiting barter or sale to the foreign trading ships. All the goods were locked securely away behind stout doors.

The speeding clouds healed the momentary tear. The sky vanished and blackness poured again upon the river and the hills.

A mile distant the city of Canton glowed dimly beside the river. A tall, gray stone wall surrounded the older part of the city. That aged barrier had been built in some misty, half-forgotten time when only a village existed there. The population had grown generation by generation to spill beyond the wall to clutter the adjoining hillsides and spread far up the river.

Pak was glad not to live in that place with its teeming throng of people and incredible maze of narrow, twisting streets. So much better to reside in the pleasant cottage in the woods near his men's barracks behind the Howqua's mansion.

It was a great honor to have obtained a contract for his squad of forty-eight warriors to guard the personal safety and possessions of one of the richest merchants in Canton. Pak's duty was to destroy quickly and skillfully any man who threatened the Howqua.

In fact, Pak's sole purpose in life was to deal violent death to others. Pak felt no fear of his own death. He had no hope of afterlife. Buddha promised nothing for him. Pak let his mind dwell on the gold and silver he received for his skill as a fighting man.

The warrior on patrol moved along the pier, passing within ten feet of his captain. Pak caught the dimmest outline of the man carrying a rifle over his shoulder. Guns were against Pak's personal code; however, he let his men use them. A strange paradox.

Pak almost shouted out at the man to scold him for not detecting the intruder standing so near. But then he held himself in check, reluctant to break the stillness.

Pak breathed deeply of the night air. He smelled the mud on the stream bank and the sour, stale odor of human waste on the water of the river. He turned away from that unpleasantness and drew in the pungent aroma of tea and sandalwood from the warehouses.

A "scrambling dragon," a trader's junk, drifted by heading downriver under the shove of its one big sail. A large flaring torch on the bow lit the way over the dark water. The men dared run the river at night so they could be at the harbor mouth to meet the British and American schooners and clipper ships at first light. The junk rounded a bend in the stream and disappeared.

Pak leaned against the mooring post and rested. Soon he would climb the hill and find his bed and sleep away the dreary hours remaining before the dawn broke.

Pak came suddenly alert, cocking his head toward the river. It came again, the faintest riffle of water around the sculling oar of a boat. He had heard such water noises far too many times to ever be mistaken about its origin. Sounds came to him of the prow of a boat cutting a small wave, followed by a series of gurgles as the disturbed river water lapped along the side of the craft.

Pak lifted the thick queue of his hair and coiled it on top of his head. With the short tassel of red silk that held the end of the braid from unraveling, he tied the mound of hair in place.

He pulled his two-edged sword from its scabbard with a whisper of steel on leather. Unknown men approaching so silently in the dark meant trouble. Honest men would have a lantern or torch. Still it was possible that someone had gotten lost on the wide body of the Pearl and his light had burned out.

"Watch out for the dock," someone whispered a warning.

The hull of the boat struck the pier with an audible thunk. A man cursed.

"Tie the boat. Make no more noise," whispered the same voice.

"Are you sure we have the correct warehouse?" asked a second man.

"I am certain. The lights on the hill are aligned perfectly. I know where we are."

Pak examined the lanterns of the Howqua's home on the high ground and the line of them lighting the private lane down to the public road. For thieves coming off the river, they were a perfect beacon for marking location. The Howqua must do without his lights in the future. It would be a difficult task to convince him of that.

"Keep your knife ready," said the first man. "These guards move on no fixed patrol. They are fierce fighters. If one discovers us, we must kill him swiftly and silently."

The two men crossed the pier, moving directly toward the middle warehouse. Pak followed, trailing them not three body lengths behind in the darkness.

Pak slowed and stopped. Let the thieves enter the warehouse, then trap and kill them there. In that way the questions of the authorities about the deaths would be easily answered.

"Keep good watch," said the first man. "I will pour oil on the hinges to keep them quiet and then unlock the door."

A man who knows the surroundings, thought Pak. One of the dock workers or warehousemen has turned thief this night.

"The key works. The door opens," whispered the first man.

"You are a sly fellow only to look at a key and then file a new one from iron."

"I have an eye for such things," boasted the first man. "But keep quiet."

The wide door swung open and the dim outlines of the men disappeared inside. Pak went forward to stop where he could peer around the edge of the doorway and into the interior.

"Here is a bundle of furs. They feel like otter pelts and are very valued. Take them quickly to the boat and hurry back."

Pak could make out the shadowy form of a man lifting up a

bulky bundle in his arms. A second figure was bending to take up another load.

Pak hissed like an angry cat. The two thieves pivoted to stare out from the murky depths of the warehouse.

Before they could unsheath their knives, Pak charged upon them. His slashing sword whistled through the air. The whistling stopped, changing abruptly to steel cutting bone and muscle.

The head of the nearest man, severed from the body, fell to the floor of the warehouse with a chatter of teeth. The body crumpled.

Pak sprang farther into the building, halted, and soundlessly went to the right a few steps. He hunched low. He heard the drip and splash of liquid puddling, and smelled the familiar, cloying odor of fresh blood.

His eyes probed the darkness, searching for the profile of the second man. There the thief was, crouched by the open door and silhouetted by the luminous glow of the lights of Canton City. He held a long-bladed knife poised to strike.

The thief was brave, but he was no night fighter to let himself be so easily seen. Pak grinned mirthlessly and sprang toward the man.

Pak's sword cut through the blackness of the night. Struck the man.

His neck was thicker than the first man's. Pak felt the difference in the swing of his weapon. Then the work of the blade was finished and the body fell away, slack and lifeless against the door. The man would never be rich stealing the Howqua's furs.

Pak stepped out into the open and gave three shrill keening calls. He hesitated a moment for the echoes between the warehouses to die, then called again in the same high pitch.

Lights came alive in the guardhouse at the far end of the wareyard. In an instant, a lantern came bobbing as a man ran swiftly in the direction of the pier. Pak nodded his approval. The man who carried the lantern was the only person visible. The two remaining warriors would be far enough to the rear to be out of the light and safe until they could locate the enemy and plan the attack. It took a brave man to carry the light.

"Over here," directed Pak.

The warrior, the light in one hand and a rifle in the other, veered and hurried up to Pak. Two other warriors came out of the dark with rifles at the ready. The guard on patrol duty raced in from the upper end of the pier. Pak noted how easily his men had adapted to firearms.

The man with the lantern held it up high to throw its yellow light across the width of the pier and into the entry of the building.

"Those two thieves broke into the warehouse," said Pak, pointing at the corpses.

"They knew what was most valuable," said one of the guards. He lifted up one of the packets of furs. "And also what was the lightest."

"Had the thieves succeeded, many elegant people would have been angry," said another guard. "There would not have been fur to line their silk robes against the winter winds." He laughed.

"The captain took two heads in the dark," said a warrior who had examined both bodies. "Look, they are cut off as neatly as if it had been an execution in full daylight. You will now surely be made regional commander of the Hung Society and have hundreds of fighters under your command." He straightened and grinned at Pak.

"What do we do with the bodies of the thieves, Captain?" asked the guard nearest the corpses.

Pak spoke to the warrior with the lantern. "Sin, go to the guardhouse where there is paper and brush and prepare a large sign. Put these words on it in red ink. 'This is the fate of all those who would attempt to steal from the Howqua.'"

"Yes, Captain," said Sin. He set the lantern down and trotted away.

Pak motioned to the remaining warriors. "Tie the thieves in the boat, one in each end so they can be seen from the river shore. Fasten the oar upright to hold the sign."

One man lit a torch and went to the boat and began to lash the oar in a vertical position. The other warriors lifted a headless corpse and carried it toward the edge of the river.

"Eeee! I am getting blood all over me," grumbled one of the men as they placed the body in the bow of the boat.

"Stop complaining," said his companion. "It will wash off. Let's go get the second body."

Sin came running back with his sign and it was fastened high up on the oar.

"Throw their heads in the boat and shove it out into the current," ordered Pak. "The Howqua may have been awakened by the disturbance. I will go and tell him his possessions are safe and we have killed two thieves."

CHAPTER 3

The dark sky lightened to gray in the east. Shortly the golden orb of the sun floated up above the Owyhee Mountains.

The bright rays of the sun struck into the valley of the Snake, drove the night shadows into the rocks and gullies and killed them there. The placid river turned to a stream of silver, and sunbeams flung brilliant arrows, glinting from the flat surface.

The heat of the rising sun penetrated the blanket encasing Tom. As the warmth replaced the chill of the night, he slept more soundly.

The sun climbed its fiery arc a handwidth. The horse grew restless and several times went off to graze, only to return to sniff at the motionless blanket wrapped body.

In the late morning, Tom awoke from a sleep of pain-filled dreams. He remained in his blanket, recalling where he was and how he had gotten there. His head felt swollen and heavy. Even though the pain still throbbed within his skull, his vision had cleared considerably.

He climbed to his feet and went to the river to kneel and drink. His thirst was old and he drank deeply. The horse followed and drank beside him.

Tom lifted the flaps of his saddlebags. His six-gun, with belt and holster was on one side. A knife in a scabbard, a small quantity of food, jerky and raisins, and a folded piece of tanned deer hide were in the other bag. Whoever had shot him had not taken all his belongings. Only his rifle and slicker were missing.

He pulled the folded section of deer hide from the saddlebag and spread the two foot width to expose a map. The neat, precise lines and symbols depicted mountains, roads, streams, and lesser features encompassing an area two hundred miles across. The most detail was portrayed for the country nearest the Alvord Desert.

Far north of the desert and beyond the badlands, the map depicted two rivers coming in from the south to join at a sharp angle. Tom read the small writing that labeled the east stream, the Snake River and the other, the Owyhee River.

Feeling relieved that he was not completely lost, Tom returned the map to the saddlebag, retrieved the blanket and climbed astride the horse. He walked the animal upstream beside the Owyhee. Where the river riffled over a gravel bar, the long-legged mount forded the current, swimming a few yards once when it could not reach bottom.

Tom guided a course north along the western side of the wide flood plains of the Snake. As the sun passed its zenith and began the long fall toward the horizon, he came onto a heavily used wagon road.

The earth had been crushed by uncounted thousands of iron-rimmed wheels over many years. In places the tracks were eroded more than a foot deep. Fresh imprints of shod hooves and wheels were pressed into the dust.

The faraway shouts of men reached Tom from the direction of the Snake. A large ferry carrying two freight wagons and six teams of horses was in the middle of the stream and heading toward his bank of the river.

Tom once again drew out his map. The much used road and the busy ferry told the importance of the route. Tom believed the road was the main traveled way connecting Fort Boise with the Oregon Country. If he was correct, the riverboat would be Feeney's Ferry.

A man on the ferry called out again. Tom spoke to his horse and went off at a fast walk without finding out what the man wanted. Until Tom was far away from the sheriff and the three dead men in Westfall, all humans must be avoided.

The road veered away from the Snake and wound up through a low range of brush covered hills and down into the flat valley of the Malheur River. The route turned beside the river and led to a score of hot springs gushing out from the base of a tall lava butte. Tom passed among the boiling pools and the steam swirling up in white columns. Following the road, he crossed the river on a solid rib of lava.

The horse plodded onward through miles of brown grass. Tom

felt the weariness grow in his weakened body. The ache in his head started to intensify and his vision became more blurred. He shook his head to clear it. At the abrupt movement, a horrible surf of pain swamped him. Earth and sky spun giddily. A series of wild disordered phantasms darted into his mind.

The impossible images commenced to merge with the reality around him. He clutched at his consciousness, straining to keep the factual sorted from the false. But they swept together, colliding and intermingling until he could not tell that which truly existed from that which did not. He grabbed at the saddlehorn to keep from falling.

The wagon master, Judson, led the line of eight freight wagons out into the shallow water near the shore of the Snake at Farewell Bend. He halted when the water rose to wash the beds of the vehicles and the bellies of the mules.

The teamsters in the high seats loosened their hold on the reins of the thirsty mules and the animals lowered their heads to drink.

While Judson waited for the teams to drink and catch their wind, he rode back past the string of wagons to inspect the equipment. Now and then he stopped to talk to one of the drivers.

At the end of the wagon train, the mounted guard shouted out to Judson, "Rider coming up behind."

The wagon master touched his mount with spurs and waded him through the water to the guard. A fast-stepping horse had crested the hill above and was drawing near.

"The fellow rides strange in the saddle," said the guard.
"Seems like maybe he's hurt," replied Judson. "Or dozing. We'll know soon for he's coming straight on."

Tom approached the wagons in the shallows of the Snake. Like a sleepwalker in whose mind a distorted version of reality exists, he saw not a wagon train in the waters of a river, but rather mules and vehicles on a flat, broad road. The mules had no legs and the wagons had no wheels. Two men sat on legless horses at the rear of the last wagon. Tom grinned crookedly—he was having a damn queer nightmare.

Judson noted blood caked in the horseman's hair and more of it crusted on his shoulder and shirt front. He spoke to Tom. "Young fellow, you look bad hurt and ready to fall from your saddle. You pull up and we'll tend your wound as best we can. Then you can ride in one of the wagons until we get to Baker. There's a doctor in that town."

Tom's grin broadened and twisted at the words of the nightmare man. "You can't help me. You have enough work to take care of your own mules and wagons." Tom laughed out loud at his joke. How could a man put legs on a mule?

Tom did not like talking to the man, an imaginary man that only existed in his head. He faced away from the bizarre gathering of deformed animals and incomplete wagons and pressed his heels into the flanks of the horse.

As he went swiftly past the wagons, Tom heard the teamsters calling out after him. He did not respond.

The guard spoke to the wagon master. "Looked like he needed help. Yet all he does is laugh and tell us to take care of our mules."

Judson watched the rider. The man's wound had bled a lot and could be serious. Yet the man spoke logically and appeared to be in good spirits.

"The fellow has left the road," said the guard. "He's heading down the Snake instead of taking the trail up the Burnt River to Baker City."

"I see he has," said the wagon master. "He's hurt and should have let us help him. There's nothing down the valley of the Snake for a hundred miles except maybe some renegade Indians."

"I've heard there's some gold miners on those big gravel bars where the Imnaha River and some smaller streams dump into the Snake."

"He'll never make it that far for he had no grub bag or gun that I could see."

"He may be out of his head. You think I should rope him and tie him in one of the wagons?"

"No. Sick or not, he's called his play. We offered our help and he turned us down. He'll live or die same as other men who have had bad luck. Now let's move the wagons out." Judson galloped his mount up out of the water of the river and onto the shore. He shouted a command at the lead wagon.

The wagon drivers popped their long bullwhips and the mules leaned into their harness. One by one the wagons crawled away from the Snake and strung out to the northwest beside the Burnt River.

Tom rode north with the current of the Snake River. As the miles were traversed, the land became steep and rose above him, soaring to tall mountains capped with pine forest. The flanks of the mountains became walls, crowding the river, funneling the large flow of water into a rushing torrent.

Tom did not know the number of days the faithful cayuse carried him beside the Snake. When the animal stopped to drink, he would dismount and drink with it. When the darkness arrived, he slept at the feet of the animal.

At times hunger gnawed at the pit of his stomach and he tried to eat some of the jerky and raisins. Each time he chewed on the food, a surge of nausea killed his desire.

Tom's head wound became infected and pus formed in the torn, mutilated flesh. Flies buzzed about and laid eggs in the corruption. Maggots came to life and fed on the rotting matter.

The periods became less frequent when his mind was clear and knew the true world. Most of the time, there was an echoing drum inside his head, the percussive beats jarring and thunderous. Images were often out of focus. In these bad times, there was only an awareness of pain and no thought. He rode by instinct, clamping the back of the horse with his legs and holding to the pommel of the saddle.

In his master's disorientation, the horse selected its own path. Once the course had been started downriver, the cayuse continued in that direction, walking steadily, making long treks each day. Neither man nor horse noted the Snake swell to a giant river as tributary after tributary added its flow, and all the tremendous volume hurried seaward.

Lian Ah swung the sickle to cut the weeds and grass in the small orchard of orange trees on the hillside above the Pearl River. Her arm was weak and a fine film of perspiration dampened her brow. She halted and leaned to rest against one of the aged fruit trees.

Her eyes ranged overhead to the hard green fruit hanging on the stiff branches. She examined every fruit within sight. A few showed a slight tinge of yellowish orange; however, many long days of growth and ripening must pass before the fruit could be eaten. She did not believe her starving body could last that long.

She stooped to her labor again. A step to the left and two strokes of the curved, hooklike blade. Then another step left and two swings. One swath after another of weeds and grass fell dead behind her as she worked the sharp sickle across the orchard.

Lian piled the wilting plants and measured the mound with a calculating eye. Two armloads at most. The plants had grown only a little since the last time she had cut them. The farmer Liexing Lip who owned the pig would give her no more than a handful of beans from his garden in exchange. Still, even a few warm beans and their broth would feel wonderful in her empty stomach. Her mouth watered at the delicious thought.

She gathered up a portion of the pig feed in her arms. Holding it tightly so not to lose one blade of grass, she carried it from the orchard and around the hill.

As she returned from the second trip with her treasure of beans, her father came into sight on the hill road. His shoulders slumped and his step was slow. His skinny body seemed to have shrunken within itself.

Lian stopped and stood motionless at the corner of the house. The expression of failure and dejection incised in her father's face squeezed her heart. He went inside without noticing her.

She moved to the window and looked inside. Her father crossed the room to the pallet on the floor where his wife lay. He brushed her pale cheek with his hand. She reached up to touch him in return.

"I found no one that needed a worker," said Gee Ah. "I offered to work a full day for just one small copper coin or a little food and still all the answers were no."

"These are terrible times," said his wife. "The drought of last year nearly destroyed the orchards on the hills. Many of the rice farmers in the valley could not get water from the river for their crops. No person has money except in the city."

"Yes. That was a bad time. But our trees that survived have fruit this year. Not a large amount because they are still weak and did not fully blossom."

"This will be a better year. We must not despair," said the wife of Gee Ah.

Lian moved away from the house. "We must not despair," her mother had said. Yet she lay starving, too frail to stand. Lian brushed at the tears that had formed and looked down from the hill toward the valley.

Hundreds of tiny orchards of closely packed trees, pear, oranges and other fruit dotted the hillside. On the bottom land of the flood plain of the Pearl River, the patchwork of rice paddies and garden plots stretched away as far as she could see.

She gazed at the location where Canton City lay. People who lived there had money. Some of them.

A slow wind drifted in from the south. The sky was clear except for a single pile of storm clouds miles away on the sea beyond the coast hills.

Lian watched the cloud mass. It appeared to be growing and moving in the direction of the land.

She gathered some twigs that had fallen from the trees in the orchard and went into the house to prepare the beans for boiling. Fifteen slender lengths of green beans, she counted. Five for each member of the family, unless her mother refused to eat as she often did.

A puff of wind darted in through the window opening. There was a bite of coolness about it. Lian went to draw a cover over her mother.

"Thank you, daughter."

"Rest and save your strength. Soon we will have a little food."

"I am not very hungry," said her mother.

"You will be when you taste how good it is."

Lian had watched the sturdy body of her mother grow thin and waste away. The bones of her chest were sharply etched through her skin. Every feeble pulse of blood was starkly visible in the blue vein in her neck.

Lian straightened and walked to the window to look outward and over the top of the orchard. The gray cloud bank had increased in size and was climbing the seaward side of the coast hills. The cloud had become darker, reminding her of the smoke that accumulated in the temple when the many candles for the dead were lighted.

"Father, the storm moves swiftly. It is coming in this direction."

Gee came to stand beside her. "This is not the season for storms. Yet, I have seen the sea grow them at odd times. It will soon die over the steep hills."

Lian did not believe this storm would die. If anything, it was growing tall and strong and its speed was quickening.

She crossed the room to the stove and added a frugal quantity of twigs to the fire beneath the beans. Then drawn by the storm, she returned to the window.

The dark clouds hurried down the landward side of the coast hills and ran along the meandering course of the Pearl River.

Lian, gripped by the inexorable march of the storm, watched it leave the valley and sweep up the front of the inland hills. It had not deviated one degree from a course directly toward her.

She stared at the intense boiling, churning gray moisture forms within the storm cloud. Did she imagine, just for a moment there in the turbulent depths, a wicked, malevolent face of some strange creature glaring out at her?

"Oh, Father, we are to be greatly harmed by the storm," cried Lian.

Before Gee Ah could answer, hail, large as the stones that boys throw, began to fall.

"Stop! Stop!" Lian shouted as the hard, white spheres crushed down upon the orchard.

The noise of the ice fall rose to a deafening roar. A thousand blows a second drummed upon the roof of the house. A million ice stones pounded the trees, shattering the limbs, beating the green fruit and stripping them from their tender hold on the mother trees.

White ice balls struck the ground and bounced high as Lian's waist. Leaves fell like crippled green butterflies. The blanket of hail on the ground built swiftly, two inches, three inches, six inches deep.

The damp wind poured into the house. Lian shivered and not all from the cold. She wrapped her arms about her breasts and swayed back and forth, emitting short moans of despair as the orchard was devastated.

She turned to her father. Their eyes met. Both began to cry. There was no need to speak what both knew. That Lian was now forfeit so that the family could survive.

The storm reluctantly ceased its ravaging of the orange trees and pulled away. The rain of hail dwindled and the size of the stones decreased.

Lian ran from the house and into the orange grove. The aftermath of destruction, the white hail, unripened fruit, and the garnish of broken limbs formed an ugly, unwholesome pudding.

Lian stomped the mixture savagely under her feet. She cursed the damnable, uncaring gods that would wreak such destruction upon innocent, blameless people. She grabbed up a broken branch and beat at the icy mass on the ground.

Finally she ceased her useless attack and looked around. Her father turned away from watching her. He walked down the hill through the melting ice toward the village.

Lian controlled her anger and sobs. The time for such emotion was past. A painful, abrupt turn had been made in her life. She threw the club from her. Never again would she curse the fates, for that was a useless action. She looked in the direction her father had gone.

In her mind's eye she could see him in the village. There on the wall of the public building, he would post a notice.

Gee Ah makes this announcement. Daughter for sale. Seventeen years. Obedient. Hard-working.

Lian wondered if he would use other words. Some fathers added pretty or beautiful. Or did her father think her ugly? He had never said.

A tiny, wizened man came early the next morning. He was standing in the yard waiting when the sun showed the round red orb of its body. He talked with her father a short time. Lian was called from the house into the yard.

The little man circled her, making brief notes on a fold of paper he carried in his hand. He nodded as if pleased by what he saw. He spoke again to Gee Ah. Reaching an understanding, they bowed to each other.

The stranger left, almost at a run.

Three days later, the old man in silk and the warrior wearing maroon cotton and a sword came to the house of Gee Ah.

CHAPTER 4

The American merchant schooner *The Orient Traveler* arrived at Lintin Island in the mouth of the Pearl River after ninety-seven days at sea. As the ship furled its sails and dropped anchor, three trading junks pulled alongside. The cargo from the foreign ship was transferred to the holds and upon the decks of the junks and lashed down. The captain of the schooner and his quartermaster went aboard one of the "scrambling dragons" and sailed upriver with its crew to Canton City.

The three riverboats tied up at a long pier on the east side of the city. The American captain immediately hired one of the Chinese seamen to deliver a packet to Yow Ho, a lawyer and elder of the Clan of Ho. Then the captain and the quartermaster went to bargain for space in one of the warehouses so they could show their cargo for bidding by the Chinese merchants.

Yow received the parcel from the seaman and went into his office. Within the packet was one thousand dollars in American gold and a message from Sigh Ho, a nephew who was far away in the Gum Shan, The Mountain of Gold, the land of California. To accompany such a large sum of money, the message was very brief:

Honorable Uncle Yow,

Buy a woman, hopefully a pretty one, and send her over the big sea to me. She would brighten my days in this strange and lonely land until I have dug my fortune from the earth and return home.

Other relatives of our family will be coming to the Gum Shan. Have one of them see that she arrives without harm. Once they have landed in San Francisco, find the merchant, Quan Ing, on Dupont Street. He will find lodging for her until I arrive. I will meet her in the time the Americans call March.

> Your Obedient Nephew,
> Sigh Ho

Yow Ho smiled. Sigh was a man of deeds and not words. Yow at once prepared an announcement that he desired to purchase a strong, young woman. He sent the message to men he knew in several villages lying at the base of the inland mountains.

On the fourth day, a dusty runner came to Yow's office. He carried word from the broker of women in the village of Hsia Pin Li. A farmer of the name Gee Ah has a daughter for sale. She is beautiful. Hurry if you wish a bargain.

Yow went immediately and spoke with Pak Ho. "I am traveling to the village of Hsia Pin Li and beyond that up into the mountains. I hope to buy a woman for your cousin Sigh. I will be carrying much gold. There are bandits in those mountains and I want you to go and keep me and the gold safe."

"Uncle, I should not leave now. Thieves are after the valuable trade goods of the Howqua. Only last night, they tried to rob him and I had to kill two of them."

"This is a family matter. It is your responsibility to accompany me."

Pak knew Yow was correct. He brushed aside thoughts of the many tasks that should be done. The duties of the warrior line of the family had been passed down from his father, and from his father's father, and before that backward into time for a hundred generations.

In these days of unrest and war, the authority of the local government administrators was weak and the Imperial authorities were far away. The fighting strength of the clan warriors was badly needed to keep the members safe from those who schemed to harm them.

Pak said, "The hill people have the most beautiful women."

"They also know the least about the true value of things. Perhaps we can buy much beauty for little money. I will hire a horse and carriage. We can leave within an hour."

"I will be ready," responded Pak. He strode off to find Sin, his second in command. That man was worthy and would make a good temporary captain of the guards of the Howqua.

Pak and Yow traveled swiftly behind the trotting horse. In the afternoon they made their way through the path of destruction cut by the storm of two days before.

Thousands of men, women and children labored in haste to level the eroded grain fields and gardens. Other thousands carried heavy baskets of mud and dumped them where once stood the dikes that held the water to flood-irrigate the crops.

The women, calling out sharp orders to the children, placed and shaped the dark brown earth. Two women began to shout at each other in disagreement over the proper locations of a farm boundary. The husbands came up, found the remnants of the previous mud wall, and the wrangle ceased.

Yow waved his arm over the toiling throng. "Like a colony of ants rushing to rebuild after their ant hill has been kicked over. I am glad to not be a farmer."

"I agree, Uncle. But they seem to endure forever. During those years when I fought in the rebellion in the Yangtze Valley, I saw ten million people slain and all the towns burned. The ravens and buzzards were so full of human flesh, they could not lift off from the ground. For days the birds merely sat among the corpses.

"When I returned a year later to the Yangtze, the country teemed with farmers. The population appeared as dense as before the killing."

"It seems that in our land the people grow from the earth. Every square inch must have a family of farmers. And life is cheap, Nephew, and you as a fighter must know that. You have slain many men."

Pak did not reply. It was not wise for a professional fighter to reflect much upon the men he had killed. Those types of thoughts could weaken the most powerful sword arm.

"Look," said Yow. He gestured ahead and off to the left to the mountains. "See the trees. A mighty hail storm has fallen there."

"I see where you mean, Uncle. And there at the bottom of the hill is Hsia Pin Li."

They met the broker of women in the village. "Do you want me to go with you?" asked the man.

"No need for that," responded Yow. "I prefer to do my own bargaining. I will pay you for your services if I make a purchase. Please tell me how to find the father of the woman."

The man pointed at a steep road leading up the flank of the mountain and gave the directions to the farm of Gee Ah.

Pak picked up the reins to start the horse. Yow laid his hand on his arm and stopped him. He spoke to the man of Hsia Pin Li. "You have not said how pretty the woman is."

"More than pretty. She is beautiful. She stirred delightful thoughts even in a man as old as I am."

Yow nodded and released his hold on Pak's arm.

Ho Pak leaned against the wall just inside the door of the house of Gee Ah. Yow Ho and the farmer sat on stools facing each other across a small wooden table. They spoke in low, polite voices, negotiating the price of Gee Ah's daughter.

Lian stood silently in the center of the room. A ray of evening sunlight shone upon the lower half of her. More of the light fell on the dirt floor and banished some of the shadows from the bleak house.

Now and then, Yow turned and openly and intently evaluated the slender girl. Pak also closely observed Lian.

She showed not the slightest awareness of either man's scrutiny. Her gaze was directed out through the open window and into the little orchard of storm-damaged orange trees.

Gee spoke to Yow. "Please allow me a moment to consider your offer."

"Time is without end," replied Yow pleasantly. The negotiation was proceeding well. The farmer would accept the offered price for he was starving. His shoulders sagged and his arms rested heavily on the table. The wife was near death on a pallet near the cold cooking hearth. It was obvious that both parents had been denying themselves food so the girl might eat. She would bring a better price with her womanly curves rounded out.

Yow glanced at Pak and did not like the expression on his face. A warrior should never show such sadness for the plight of others.

Pak appraised the girl. Her black hair was drawn loosely back to fully expose the delicate curves and planes of her face. Her lips were full and curved neither up nor down. A mouth set firmly to meet an unpredictable and often violent world. The eyes were exceptionally large and almost black. Altogether a lovely countenance.

She was below average height. Her slender body was clothed in a yellow silk blouse and trousers. Pak wondered where such a poor family had obtained the price of silk garments. However, they were not new, but rather appeared of an old fashion. Were they some long-hidden treasure of the mother, secreted away for a joyous trip one day? Instead, now to be used to display the beauty of her daughter for sale to unknown men?

Without conscious thought, Pak drew a deep breath. He smelled the old mud and grass that made the bricks of the walls of the house. The odor of the dead ashes in the open hearth of the kitchen wafted to him. A pleasant scent of a flower teased him. There were no flowers near the house. Had the girl obtained some blossoms and crushed them on her skin?

"Lian is my only child," said Gee, once again starting the bargaining. "There will be no one to bring laughter into my home after she is gone."

"A daughter is very pleasant in an old man's life," said Yow. "However, a son is more helpful."

Yow reached into the folds of his clothing and brought out a leather pouch. He methodically extracted one fifty dollar gold piece at a time and placed four of them in a row on the table in front of the farmer.

Gee said, "She has never known a man. This amount of gold you offer is not enough. It should be twice as much."

Yow looked penetratingly at Lian. She felt his stare and turned to gaze at him.

Pak watched the young woman meet the inquisition of the skilled negotiator. Her intelligent eyes, wide and luminous, did not waver. Her shoulders squared, pulling her blouse tight, imprinting the mounds of her bosom in the soft yellow silk.

Pak saw the beauty of Lian. He sensed the strength of her. His heart thudded within the cage of his chest—a strange reaction, for she meant nothing to him.

Stranger still, he found himself speaking. "Honorable Uncle, pay the price they have asked."

Startled, Yow spun around. Anger flashed through him at the unheard of interruption. He was head of the Ho Clan. It was his duty to obtain the greatest value at the least cost. His tongue curled to lash out at the impudent Pak.

Yow caught himself. Pak was a powerful man in his own right. He was rising swiftly up through the ranks of the Triad warriors. In a recent battle in the hills above Canton, Pak had killed fourteen men in hand-to-hand combat. From a boy warrior in the Tai Ping rebellion, he had advanced now to a position where, with one word, he could summon half a hundred fighters. They would willingly go to their deaths upon his command.

"Pay them, great Uncle," said Pak. "I will explain the price to Sigh myself."

Yow said to Gee Ah, "Our young people speak when, in times past, it would have been unthinkable. But perhaps it is proper. Soon they will be the elders and must set the course and resolve the problems of the family."

Yow brought out the leather pouch again. "Four hundred American dollars. A fortune." He began to count gold coins out on the table.

Lian looked at the Ho fighter. She had been surprised at his outburst. He was taller than either her father or the elder Ho. His face was long, with large, somewhat bulbous eyes. They returned her examination with a steady, curious expression of their own.

A two-inch scar marred the left side of his face at the jaw bone. A smaller scar was above the left eye socket. Slightly lower and the blade making that injury would have blinded one eye.

His maroon clothing was cut more closely to his body than was the normal style, almost like a uniform. The column of his neck appeared strong, the muscles standing out like strong cords beneath his skin. His hands were broad and muscular, with callouses on knuckles and fingertips from thousands of strikes upon the toughening block. The mark of a fierce Triad fighter. She felt a shiver at the deadliness evident in him.

Yow extracted a roll of paper from an inner pocket. He separated the two sheets and spread them on the table. A brush and ink followed. Yow and Gee signed the contract.

"It is done, Lian," said her father.

"Yes, Father. I am very happy. Buy yourself a larger orchard and hire a poor peasant to work for you. Have the tailor in the village sew you new clothing. Then go and join the elders in study. Send mother to visit her people in Foochow."

Gee arose and quickly went outside. Pak saw the hint of tears in the man's eyes as he passed.

"I will get my belongings," said Lian. She was now in bondage for life to the family Ho and was expected to go immediately and live with the elder man until he told her what was to be her task. She stooped and went through the low entry into a small adjoining room.

Pak moved to stand beside Yow. "You did not tell them she was to go on the long journey to the Land of Golden Hills."

"That would have driven up the price. Even more than you so recklessly did."

Yow led the way into the yard and stopped near Gee. Pak followed. No one spoke, each thinking his private thoughts.

Lian came outside with her sleeping pallet and bundle of clothing. She had changed her garb to cotton. She took a carrying pole from where it leaned against the side of the house and tied the pallet to one end and the clothing to the other.

"Honorable Ho, may I have another minute before we leave?" asked Lian.

Yow nodded his approval. Lian walked to the edge of the orchard.

She stroked the rough bark of the nearest orange tree. She laid her forehead against the knotted bole. After a moment, she raised her head and her sad eyes roamed their tender touch over the ancient orchard.

"Goodby old friends," she whispered.

Returning to the men, Lian stood in front of her father. "Send me news of yourself often, Father."

Gee Ah reached out a hand and felt the splendid cheek of his daughter. "And you, too, Lian. Send news often." He backed away, and as if very tired, leaned against the wall of the house for support.

Pak and Yow walked from the yard and toward their carriage standing in the rutted road. Lian shouldered her carrying pole, and with the two opposite weights swaying to her steps, fell in behind the two men.

The men took the only seat. Lian placed her scant possessions in the rear of the vehicle and climbed in to sit on her rolled sleeping pallet. She did not believe she would ever see her home again.

Pak clucked at the horse and it moved off with the wagon along the road leading down the hill to the river bottom.

CHAPTER 5

In the weak light of a thin, new moon, the weary black horse carrying Tom Gallatin came onto a long gravel bar beside the Snake River. Its iron-shod hooves grated on the round stones. One round rock rolled and the horse stumbled.

Tom's slack body pitched from the saddle and fell upon the hard stones. He did not stir. The damp November cold of the river settled over him.

Sigh Ho arose from his sleeping pallet on the floor. In the pitch blackness of the cabin, he took his coat from a peg driven in a log of the wall and moved along the aisle between the two rows of slumbering men.

He accidentally brushed against one of the sleepers and that person, disturbed in some private dream, murmured a few unintelligible words and then his voice trailed off.

The door opened silently on its leather hinges and Sigh went outside. He glanced at the nearby cookhouse and farther away the second sleeping cabin. Not a glimmer of light showed that would indicate the occupants were awake. As was usual, Sigh had arisen first.

He moved away from the crude log structure and looked out over the Snake River Valley. The mighty chasm lay full of black night to its rim. The wet, rumbling noise of the turbulent flow of the river through its rocky, two-hundred-yard-wide gorge reached him. Overhead a multitude of stars were tiny pricks of light in the dark heavens.

Against the faint starshine in the east, Sigh traced the two mile high angular peaks of the Seven Devils Mountains. Towering only slightly lower, the round dome of Black Mountain lay close on the west side of the river. This foreign land was raw and wild.

Somehow that seemed to Sigh to be a fitting place to find his fortune.

The first year of Sigh's sojourn in America, he had worked in California, on the North Fork of the American River in the Cascade Mountains. Unlike nearly all Chinese who avoided contact with the Americans as much as possible, he had deliberately sought a job with them so he could learn their difficult language and, more importantly, study the most profitable technique for finding and working the gold deposits.

In the early summer of the second year, Sigh had gathered thirty-one of his countrymen, mostly from Kwangtung Province like himself, and had followed the tales of the new gold strike in Oregon. They had twice stopped to work on the Central Pacific Railroad to earn money for supplies and food. By late summer they had crossed the harsh desert of Nevada and reached the valley of the Snake River.

They spread along the river and for several days worked downstream, panning the gravel bars of the main stream and testing all the side tributaries for gold concentration. At the base of Black Mountain, where a steep, tumbling stream emptied into the Snake, they had encountered the white man, Ed Cason. He had staked his claim to a long gravel bar on the west side of the river and was beginning a one-man mining operation.

Cason offered the little army of men a share of the claim to help remove the overburden to reach the gold he believed lay buried near the contact zone between the fluvial material and the ancient bedrock. Before Sigh would agree to the proposal, he selected six members of his crew who were skilled at washing gold and they prospected up the creek that was the source for the sand and gravel on the bar.

Because of the steepness of the bed of the stream, little sedimentary material was present to examine. However, Sigh found a golden nugget weighing a quarter ounce wedged in a crack in a rock. They searched diligently to discover another nugget or the origin of the first. They located neither.

Returning to the river, they had discussed the single find with those of their crew who had stayed behind. They questioned whether or not that was the only gold in all the eroded land. Or was it a symbol left to guide them to great wealth?

In the end, the Chinamen pooled their scant money and made a counteroffer to Cason. They would purchase his claim for eleven hundred dollars.

Cason had mined gold from a score of placer diggings and with that experience had thoroughly studied the shape and depth of this gravel bar. Many of the stones were large and could not be washed away by redirecting part of the river flow. Further he had determined the bedrock dipped steeply and lay deep beneath the overburden. Many hundreds of tons of heavy stones and ten times that much sand and gravel would have to be shouldered and carried away to expose the bedrock.

The white man accepted the offer of the small brown men and producing his record of the filing of his claim at Baker, signed it over to one Sigh Ho and thirty-one other, unnamed Chinamen.

Immediately Sigh and his comrades began to construct two log sleeping cabins and a cook shack on a narrow bench above the flood zone of the river. The cottonwood trees cut easily and the structures were soon erected. Not too soon for the anxious men. Below them, awaiting their eager hands, was a gravel bar some two hundred feet long and fifty feet wide. The gods be willing, buried in that sedimentary mass would be a golden treasure awaiting Sigh and his comrades. They would all return to China as rich men.

Sigh saw the morning dusk arrive on the top of the mountains and begin to descend onto the valley. Objects began to take form. Sigh heard the cook arise and start his fire.

The twilight sank downward, brightening the darkness in the bottom of the valley. Hidden objects took form. Sigh saw a gaunt black horse standing on the gravel bar and a man sprawled on the rocks.

Sigh ran quickly to the nearest cabin and shook the sleeper nearest the door.

"What do you want? Is it time to get up?" questioned the man.

"Wake all the others," directed Sigh. "There is a stranger near the river and we must find out what he is doing here."

Sigh alerted the cook and sent him to wake the men in the second sleeping cabin.

All the men assembled hurriedly and followed Sigh down the bank to the gravel bar. The horse heard their approach over the rock and turned to face them. It snorted loudly, warning the men off.

Sigh stopped and studied the man lying in an unnatural crumpled slackness. He was either unconscious or dead.

Sigh moved forward slowly, speaking in a low, soothing voice to the horse standing protectively over the inert figure. The animal laid back his ears and bared his teeth like a big guard dog.

"Maybe we should wait until the horse leaves," suggested one of the men.

"Or throw rocks and drive him away," said another.

"No," responded Sigh. "Stay close and be silent. We are not afraid of one horse, even if he does act fierce."

The black animal gave way, retreating reluctantly step by step before the press of men.

Sigh spoke to Yuen, the healing man of the group. "Check the white man's condition."

The healer knelt and placed his ear to Tom's chest. "He lives."

Yuen felt Tom's legs and arms and found them sound. He unbuttoned the ragged shirt and ran his practiced hands along Tom's body. The ribs stuck out painfully bony, like ripples of sand beneath the skin. None were broken. He parted the hair stiff with old blood and examined the head injury.

"He has no broken bones," said Yuen. "There are bruises from falling. Some are old, some new. He has a very bad wound on the head. Probably been shot. It is badly infected. Without cleaning it, I cannot tell if the skull is broken or not."

Sigh had been scanning up and down the river. No other men or horses were present in either direction before the river curved away out of sight. He believed the white man had accidentally stumbled upon their camp. He stepped to the horse, now quiet and watching closely, and searched through the saddle bags.

Finishing his inspection of the articles he had found on the horse, Sigh spoke to Yuen. "Can you save his life?"

"The head wound is the worst. It is several days old and he still lives. Therefore, there is reason to believe he will not die from that. But sometimes wounds such as this upon the head leave the man addled in thought. We could not know if that will be this man's fate until we hear him speak."

Sigh pondered the situation a moment longer. Then he spoke to the group of men gathered around him.

"We will help the man to live. Two of you carry him to the cabin where Yuen sleeps. He will heal him if it is possible."

"No! That is not what we should do," exclaimed a tall man standing in the center of the crowd. "We should take what we need of the foreign devil's things and throw him in the river."

"Scom, we are not thieves or murderers," responded Sigh.

"Maybe not yet," Scom's voice was tight with challenge. "But what have white men ever done for us except to treat us worse than dogs in the street and tax us outrageously for digging gold? I say we do not help this man."

"We may have need of him," said Sigh. "If he recovers he will be in our debt. I have thought of ways he could aid us. Ways in which we cannot help ourselves."

"He means nothing to us now and never will in the future. Who of you are with me? We will take the horse to carry supplies from Baker City and drag the boulders from the gravel bar so we can get to the gold. Since Sigh does not want us to kill the white man, we will simply let him die by himself. He looks nearly dead now."

A few men near him growled ominously in agreement. They moved forward in a knot, elbowing aside those in the way.

A large man who had been standing attentively in the rear, now hastily circled the throng. He stopped near Sigh and spoke to him. "I would like to give my help to you. Those mean fellows are strong and might try to use force to have their way."

Sigh looked up at the big man. Yutang was a brave and ferocious fighter. "I welcome your offer. I do not want anyone hurt. If there is to be trouble, let them start it."

"And then I shall end it." Yutang spread his large hands and grinned.

Yutang pivoted to face the men. "I side with Sigh. He organized this venture to find gold. There can be only one leader. We have selected Sigh. He says he has a way to use this man and I believe it would be a good plan."

Yutang hesitated for a moment then began to speak again. "Scom is one who always disagrees and causes trouble among us. Do not listen to him."

Yutang ranged his sight over the gathering to see how his words were being taken. Scom and his cohorts were still moving forward, but they had slowed. Unless some of the uncommitted men supported Sigh quickly, there would be a fight.

"Yutang is correct," said a man who had just been shoved by Scom.

Many heads nodded and a loud murmur of voices rose to declare Sigh was the man to follow.

"They had better let this end and not get Yutang mad," said a man. He laughed as if he hoped there would be a battle.

"You are all making a big mistake," said Scom scornfully.

"You have had your chance to speak and only your cronies back you," said Sigh. "We will do this as I say." He was sorry to see the division among the men. That could only weaken the group.

Yutang bent and scooped Tom's thin body up effortlessly in his arms. "I do not need assistance to carry the man to the cabin."

Scom stood directly in Yutang's path. As the big man with his burden drew close, Scom's comrades warily moved aside. Scom spread his legs and put his hands on his hips.

"Get out of my way," ordered Yutang in a harsh voice. "If you cause me trouble, I will break your head and you will be the one that goes into the river instead of the white man."

Scom's eyes, dark and furtive, slid away and he stepped from in front of Yutang.

"Lay him outside where the sunlight will shine on him so I can see to work," Yuen called to Yutang and trailed him up to the cabin and knelt beside Tom.

Yuen ignored the fetid stench of decaying flesh and brushed the white maggots from the grave injury on Tom's head. With soap and water and a soft cloth, he washed away the yellow pus and dirty brown corruption. He did not stop until all the wound was exposed and oozing fresh blood from the raw, pink edges.

When the wound lay clean, Yuen assessed the damage that had been done by the strike of the bullet on the head. A shallow groove, long as his finger, creased the skull. He nodded with satisfaction: the bone had shattered away under the impact and the skull was not caved inward to crowd the brain.

"How bad is it?" asked Sigh, who sat nearby and watched.

"It is a very severe wound. But he is young. More than that I cannot say. Now while he is still unconscious and cannot feel the pain, I must close the opening. You hold the flesh together and I will do the stitching.

Yuen spread a thin coating of salve from a small glass bottle over the injury. Then deftly with a curved needle and fine silk thread, he started his task. Sigh observed the needle pierce the flesh and the thread draw the lips of the wound snugly against each other. He was always amazed at the skill of the healer.

As if sensing Sigh's thoughts, Yuen said, "The scar will not be much, but there will be a sunken area where some of the bone is missing. However, it will be covered by his hair."

Yuen finished and again spread a film of salve over the stitched scalp. "Only time will answer our questions of how completely he will heal. That might be days or weeks. In the meantime, he must be fed and tended. It will require a great deal of effort."

"If I am correct in my plan, his help to us will be worth all the care we provide him."

"What is your plan?" asked Yuen.

Sigh climbed to his feet and without answering went off toward the gravel bar and the men working there.

Tom came awake, floating up from the dark pit of unconsciousness. He lay stretched out on his back. A pleasant feeling of warmth bathed his body and his head was free of pain.

With great joy he realized his mind was clear.

He sensed its capacity to create order out of disorder, to discard the false dredges of his past hallucinating dreams.

He allowed his thoughts to wander backward through the passageways of his memories. A kaleidoscope of past events tumbled through his mind, stopping for a moment at significant scenes.

He remembered the violence he had done and the three dead men in Westfall. He recalled running before the sheriff and his deputies. He meant the lawmen no harm, wanting only to stay far out in front of them and go to a safe place.

Then he had found the hurt deputy and helped him off the lava. That had ended with a period of blackness the length of which he did not know. The cold rain had awakened him and he had made the brain-jarring and seemingly endless ride beside a large river.

There were unknown hours and days associated with that pain-filled journey. Some of the missing sections might never be filled. However, remembrances of that time were surfacing even now, fragments of it drifting up like a spark from the dark hole of a chimney to add another bit to form a more complete picture.

He was awake from his nightmare and knew he was finished with it. He was no longer locked within his head and he felt the ebb of his life running strong and vital.

The facts of this new situation must be quickly sorted out. Tom opened his eyes a crack and peered out. He lay on the ground in the sun. Mountain peaks covered with pine forest loomed above him on all sides, piercing the clear blue sky that arched overhead. The bottom quarter or so of the mountain slopes were carpeted with brown grass dotted here and there with patches of green brush and an occasional dark brown outcrop of granite. Below him at the base of a short, steep incline, a large river sped swiftly past between curving boulder-strewn banks. On a gravel bar beside the rushing water, many men worked.

They were small men with brown skin. All were dressed in dark blue shirts and pants. Most wore hats, conical straw ones. Long braids of hair hung down each man's back. Tom saw broad shaven areas on the front of the men's heads.

Tom watched the men labor. Eight of them, working in pairs, carried large stones off the gravel bar in canvas slings hanging between two long poles they rested on their shoulders. Twice that many men with shovels and baskets were transporting the smaller stones. All material was carried out into the flow of the river and dumped there.

Two gold sluice boxes were situated in the edge of the water at each end of the bar. A man at each box shoveled sand and gravel into the upper end of the riffled sluice. Two men scooped water up in buckets and flushed the sand and gravel down the corrugated channel.

A small young man went from one sluice box to the other, and with a metal blade, scraped the material trapped between each riffle into a bucket. This accumulation he carried to a man squatting on a flat stone near the edge of the river.

That man took a quantity of the substance and placed it in a shallow pan some eighteen inches across. Then, dipping water and swirling the mixture, he winnowed the heavy yellow sediment and allowed the lighter to wash away into the river.

Tom watched the workers repeating the rhythm and cycle of their tasks over and over. Rarely did they spreak and even then he could not hear because of the distance and the sound of the rushing water.

Who were they? Were they enemies? Tom began to organize his thoughts for a scheme to deal with the strange men.

Tom very cautiously rolled his head to look for his horse. The black mount was foraging in the willows and cottonwoods downriver from the miners.

A step sounded on the ground beside Tom. He hastily shut his eyes and lay very still.

A man's hand caught him by the throat. The fingers pressed inward, not hard, merely feeling, testing. The man shouted loudly in some language Tom did not understand.

Instantly, the men stopped working. All except four surged up the bank en masse.

"He is awake," said Yuen. "His heart beats fast. He only acts unconscious."

"That is exactly what I would do," said Sigh. "But now it is time to talk with him. I hope I know enough of his language to make my meaning clear."

"Come awake," Sigh said in heavily accented English.

Tom opened his eyes. Many round, brown faces surrounded him. Black eyes stared intently.

"Hello," said Sigh. "You understand me?"

"Yes," responded Tom.

"That is good. You have been with us four days. We have waited."

Tom strained to comprehend the broken and almost unintelligible words. The tone sounded friendly. He relaxed slightly.

He placed his hands on the ground and tried to sit up. He could not lift the weight of his body.

"Your strength will return," said Yuen.

Sigh said to Tom, "Yuen says you will become strong. He is the one that helped you to life."

Tom looked at Yuen. "Thank you. I am in your debt."

A pleased expression swept over Sigh's face. He leaned and

caught hold of Tom's shoulders. "Let me help you sit up. Are you hungry?"

"Starved." Tom realized he had never wanted food so badly.

"Then you shall eat," Sigh called out to the cook. "Hoy, bring something nourishing for our new friend."

A moment later, a bowl of soup was placed in Tom's hand. His weakened body trembled in anticipation of the food. His hand shook as he spooned a bit into his mouth.

The aroma teased his nostrils and the flavor tingled his tongue. His stomach welcomed the delicious soup. He chewed slowly, savoring every tidbit.

Never afterward would Tom be able to describe the contents of the mixture, for his mind was occupied with the realization he would live. That knowledge gave the food an essence that never again could be duplicated.

"What is your name?" asked Sigh.

"Tom Gallatin."

"I am Sigh Ho. You will get to know the others later. Are you alone?"

"Yes. All alone."

"Then you shall stay with us awhile. Rest now. We have much work to do. We will talk again when the sun has gone down and it is dark." Sigh said something to the men that Tom did not understand and all filed away to the river.

Tom saw heavy scowls on the faces of the four men who had not come up the bank at Yuen's call. He wondered why they appeared to be angry.

CHAPTER 6

Tom lay in the gentle afternoon warmth of the November sun. Now and then he lifted his head and watched the Chinamen laboring on the gravel bar. He was amazed at the men's relentless assault on the huge river deposit. Only rarely did a man stop to rest and then only for a moment.

The men were young, most under thirty. All but two were small, hardly more than five feet tall and weighing less than one hundred and twenty pounds. The exceptions were a handwidth taller than the others. One of the two was striking in that he was unnaturally broad, greater by more than twice any of his comrades.

He was one of the pair of men who carried the largest stones from the bar in the pole and canvas slings. Three times during the day Tom had noted a fresh worker relieve the mate of the man, for no one could maintain the rigorous pace he set.

On the upstream end of the bar where the alluvium was the thinnest, the men had exposed the granite bedrock for a stretch of thirty feet or so. One of the younger Chinamen was flushing the fractured granite surface with buckets of water and examining the material wedged in the cracks.

He stooped and grabbed up something in his hand. For a few seconds he turned it in the sunlight. Then he cried out shrilly and began to laugh and dance about. He thrust the object high above his head and ran to Sigh.

The others speedily surrounded Sigh and the young man. They milled and shoved to see what had been found. Their laughter and shouts of delight rose above the noise of the river and echoed against the far mountainside.

The joy of the Chinamen drew Tom. He climbed shakily erect and went down the bank to join the happy throng.

On the palm of Sigh's hand lay a golden cube of gold approximately three inches on each side. The corners of the malleable metal had been slightly rounded from being tumbled by the running waters. The cube's journey from its birthplace had been short.

Sigh handed the square of yellow metal to the nearest man. "Pass it around. Let everyone feel it for luck. There may be many more of these buried beneath the gravel."

The man hefted the lump of gold in his hand. "It weighs many ounces. This one piece alone will make several of us rich."

"It could buy many things in China," agreed the man beside him and took the gold.

The cube of precious metal passed from man to man. Each stroked and caressed it with his calloused fingers. Tom wondered what their dreams were.

One man made as if to put it in his pocket and then laughed at the others as they let out a roar of disapproval.

Sigh recaptured the gold and placed it atop a large rock in the middle of the gravel bar. "We can all see it there. Now back to work. We may soon find another to match this one."

He silently decided that when the gravel bar had been fully sifted for all its wealth, he would search again for the mother lode, the source of the gold. There had to be one place where the golden fluids from deep in the earth had been concentrated. What a glorious discovery that would be.

The yellow ball of the sun dropped behind the peak of Black Mountain and shadows filled the deep Snake River Valley. The wind began to blow chilly.

On the gravel bar, one of the Chinamen ceased working and, taking his basket, set off downstream along the shore of the river. An hour later he returned with the basket full of fish. The man must have a fish trap, thought Tom, or several baited hooks set in the river.

Hoy took the fish and went up the slope to the cook shack. The fisherman turned back to his work on the bar.

Tom saw smoke from Hoy's cooking fire begin to rise from the chimney. He considered joining the man, for the cold wind was cutting through his thin cotton shirt. Still, Tom had not been invited inside, so he remained on the river bank.

When the shadows were dark with evening dusk, Hoy rang a

high-pitched metal bell from the door of the cookhouse. At the
signal an instant change occurred in the laboring men. Their
quietness broke and they began to talk to each other. Quickly
they stowed their shovels, buckets and slings.

Taking time only to remove their boots, they rushed into the
river, submerging themselves completely. They surfaced, blowing noisily and swinging their long wet queues heavy with river
water. Speedily they stripped and bathed, using fine sand from
the bottom of the river to wash away the grime of the day's work.

The men scrubbed their sweaty clothing and wrung the water
from them. Then trooped unabashedly naked up the slope to
their sleeping quarters. Shortly they emerged in dry blouses and
pants and filed into the cookhouse. Tom was to learn this was an
evening ritual of the Chinamen except when the ice locked the
river away under its white barrier.

He thought the bathing an excellent idea and checked his own
clothing. They were filthy. He went to the river and in a pool of
more quiet water in an eddy behind a large boulder, washed his
garments and bathed.

He tugged the wet trousers and shirt on. In the cold wind, they
felt like ice. He shivered. Unless a person had a change of dry
garments, maybe it wasn't such a good thing to become wet. Yet
even cold, the cleanliness felt remarkably fine. He walked up
from the river to the cookhouse and peered inside.

Sigh came to meet him. "I saw you in the river. Here is some
dry clothing. Put them on and then come inside."

"Thank you," said Tom. He stood beside the wall of the cabin
and changed into a set of Chinaman's blue pants and blouse. His
arm protruded a good six inches from the sleeves of the shirt and
his legs an equal distance from the legs of the pants. He felt so
warm and comfortable that he smiled with pleasure. Stooping
low, he passed through the short doorway and went inside.

The cookhouse was crowded with the gathering of Chinamen.
Hoy worked at several pots set in the hot coals of an open fire-
place. All the others sat on low benches on opposite sides of a long
table made of split logs, the flat side up.

Four tallow candles were spaced along the table and dimly lit
the interior of the room. The yellow flames, flickering in the wind
drafts from the open doorway, threw wavering shadows upon all

the round, brown faces, the partially shaved heads and the black eyes. The men stared back at Tom with fixed expressions.

In the half light in the crude log cabin on the wild Snake River, the men looked very alien to Tom. The thoughts behind their eyes were unfathomable. Still, he nodded a greeting and smiled at them for they had treated his wound and given him food and warm clothing.

"Sit here beside me," said Sigh and motioned at a vacant space.

"You are very hospitable to a stranger," said Tom.

"What you mean hospitable?" asked Sigh, unfamiliar with the word.

"Very kind," explained Tom.

Sigh laughed at the compliment. "Yes. I think you would be kind to us also." He believed what he said. He sensed a gentleness about the white man, one who spoke in an odd way, each word deliberately and distinctly spoken as if he were placing something fragile upon a hard surface.

Sigh lifted a cloth-wrapped bundle from the bench and handed it to Tom. "All your possessions are in here. I took them from your horse."

"Thank you," said Tom.

His tanned deer hide map was there. He smoothed it with his hands, glad it had not been lost. Also, there were his knife in a scabbard, a small quantity of jerky and raisins and his six-gun. He pulled the pistol from its holster and found it had been cleaned and lightly oiled.

"You have taken good care of my things," said Tom. "It seems I am much in your debt. Not only for these things, but for my very life. I am not sure that I will ever be able to repay you."

Sigh spoke swiftly to his countrymen in their language. Then he turned to Tom. "I told them what you said. You are among friends here. Rest awhile with us. When you are strong, there is more than enough work for all of us on the gravel bar. There may come a time when you can help us in other ways."

Tom did not understand all of the heavily accented English words. Nevertheless he comprehended enough to know the meaning of the man's statement. He smiled his pleasure and agreement.

"The food is ready," said Hoy. He lifted the large pots from the fire and set them directly onto the table.

A stack of tin plates were speedily distributed. Tin cups and chopsticks and a scattering of forks and knives followed. All began to eat.

Tom ate the food with high relish. He knew the men watched him eat. That did not lessen his wolfish forage upon the food. He reached for a third helping of the boiled brown beans, tender flesh of the river fish, and some substance with a crunchy texture.

"The foreign devil eats like a pig," exclaimed Scom in a cutting voice. "Already he has consumed as much food as three of us. Twice as much as Yutang. We cannot afford his help. It is difficult to haul the supplies from Baker City."

At the explosion of rapid words, Tom stopped dipping the food onto his plate. He did not understand the man's language, but the expression of anger and resentment on Scom's face fully told the man's feelings. Tom let the ladle fall back into the pot.

He looked past the rows of faces of the men at the stock of provisions on shelves along the rear wall and on the floor. There were cans, jars, boxes and sacks of what he believed to be food stuff. Still, compared with the large number of men, the quantity of provisions were very inadequate. There was indeed something for all to worry about. Winter could begin any day and they could be locked for weeks in the mountain valley.

Tom turned to Sigh. He must apologize for his lack of consideration of the needs of the men who helped him.

The Chinaman spoke more quickly. "It is understandable that you are very hungry. Scom should not have spoken as he did. I am sorry for his rudeness. Now finish your food for you are welcome here."

Scom grunted once in disagreement and lapsed into silence. Tom saw the hatred in the Chinaman's eyes, ageless and ugly. Scom flung a last malignant glance at him and sprang up from the table and went out through the door into the darkness.

Tom awoke with the first paling of the stars. He left the cabin where he had slept on a pallet near Yuen and walked quietly south along the course of the river. He did not see Sigh sitting on the rock above the river. The Chinaman noted Tom passing.

Sigh reentered the cabin and woke Yutang. "The white man has gone up the river. Follow without being seen and find out what he does."

"You do not trust him? Do you think he has a scheme to steal our gold?"

"I do not know what plan he might have. We will watch him closely."

"How long ago did he leave?"

"Just now. Be very careful."

The game trail came down from the pine forest on the high, humpbacked reaches of Black Mountain. It zigzagged back and forth across the nearly vertical slope, avoiding several rock out-croppings and the hazardous talus slopes below them, and ended at the Snake. Three buck deer, heads sprouting heavy antlers with sharp ivory tines, moved in sure-footed agility along the path.

Tom lay hidden on a small brush-covered point of land near the river and overlooking the game trail. He watched the deer de-scend the flank of the mountain, stopping briefly at times to nibble a bud from a bush, or to stand for a longer period, ears flicking first in one direction and then another for sound, and eyes scouring the terrain ahead.

The wind was still the night wind, falling down the slope to the colder valley bottom. It flowed away from the deer and to Tom and they did not know of his presence.

He had spotted the tell-tale scar of the trail on the mountain-side the day before while he had lain resting on the river bank. The ease with which he had located it from nearly a quarter mile had told him it was well-used. After the incident of the food, he had vowed to kill a deer to replenish what he had eaten.

Silently Tom drew his six-gun from its holster. Not a fitting weapon for killing a deer unless it was very close.

He had considered asking Sigh for the loan of a rifle. However, not one gun was visible among the entire group. It appeared the Chinamen had come into the hostile land without weapons other than knives. That could prove to be a fatal error.

Tom mentally measured the range to the game trail and judged it sixty feet. Careful aim must be taken to hit a vital spot.

Tom waited in his ambush, enjoying the challenge of the hunt. As the dawn gradually brightened, he examined his intended prey.

The lead buck was past the prime of his life; the normally gray-brown pelage was almost white on muzzle and chest. The other two were young and sleek.

The deer came closer, a mere two hundred feet distant. The old buck stopped and the two trailing animals halted close behind. The lead buck looked directly at the brush patch where Tom lay. His head rose and the black openings of his nostrils flared, sucking air, testing for scent.

You are a wise bugger—that is why you have lived so long, thought Tom. But come a little nearer.

The wary animals remained frozen, like pewter statues. The minutes slid by. Sunlight touched the evergreen forest on the top of Black Mountain.

The younger bucks impatiently shoved past the aged one and came forward on the trail. Well, you smart old rascal you are safe, thought Tom. He extended his pistol and sighted along the barrel at the closest deer.

The six-gun boomed. The speeding bullet shattered a rib, drove inward to pierce the throbbing heart.

Instantly Tom rotated his point of aim, seeking the second deer. That animal had spun away from the sound of the gun and was facing up the river. It sprang mightily, launching itself into a twenty-foot leap.

Tom triggered the six-gun, striking the buck a glancing blow on the back of the head. It crashed down, a pile of slack muscle and jumbled legs. The deer pulled itself together and struggled to its feet. Tom took deliberate aim and broke its neck with a shot.

A second later, a shout sounded nearby. Yutang came out of a pocket of brush and hurried to Tom.

Yutang smiled broadly as he surveyed the dead deer. He pointed at the location of the bullet holes and nodded his understanding of the skill required to place them exactly so to make the kill.

Tom was angry at the presence of the man. The deer could

have easily been spooked and his opportunity to supply meat and repay the Chinamen would have been lost.

Yutang brought a knife from inside his blouse and began to remove the entrails of one of the animals. Now and then as he worked, he laughed happily, his deep bass chuckles sounding like rocks rolling down a rough stone canyon.

Tom's anger faded at the evident pleasure and approval of the big Chinaman. He pulled his own knife and started to gut the second deer.

When they had finished with the deer, Yutang lifted one to his shoulder. He said something to Tom and gestured at the remaining carcass. Then he hesitated, glancing at Tom's thin, half-starved body. Yutang did not wait for Tom to take up the deer, but bent and caught the animal by the base of an antler. Carrying one deer, and dragging another, he moved off toward the cabins.

Tom was glad the big man had the load for he did not believe he could have lifted one of the deer. He walked behind Yutang, feeling the ancient atavistic joy of the successful hunter giving him strength to keep up.

At the evening meal, Tom ate a huge quantity of venison stew and hot bread. He finished, smiled his thanks at Hoy for a fine meal, and went outside to sit on the ground by the cabin wall.

Sigh also came outdoors and took a seat beside Tom. They sat without speaking, listening to the yellow moon come up.

Sigh broke the quietness and asked in a shy voice, "Can you teach me to read and write the English?"

Tom nodded and smiled, pleased and moved by the strange warmth of having something unique to give to this man who had shown him so much kindness. "I would be glad to do that if you would teach me to speak your language. And tell me the customs of your country."

"Good. Shall we start now?" asked Sigh.

"Never too early to begin. What word should be the first?"

"Friend," said Sigh.

"Yes. Friend is a good word."

They went back inside. Sigh found pencil and paper. They studied at the table in the candleshine. The moon rose the height of a tall man before the lesson ended and the two men found their pallets on the floor of the cabin and went to sleep.

CHAPTER 7

Tom's head had no pain on the second day and he worked with the Chinamen on the gravel bar. He filled his basket only a third full of stones, but even so he had to rest often. His legs were wobbly with fatigue by the time Hoy rang his bell for supper.

Tom ate mightily that night. The evening language lesson with Sigh was short. He slid off to sleep listening to Sigh repeating the word "bill of sale."

The following morning several of the men did not go to work on the gravel bar. Instead they assembled by the cookhouse and made ready for a journey.

Sigh spoke to Tom, "Wong and nine others are going to Baker City to buy our winter supplies. May they use your horse? With it they can bring back a much larger quantity of provisions."

"They are welcome to take him," said Tom. "Tell Wong he must keep hold of the horse or keep him tied, for at the first chance he will leave them and come back to me."

Sigh talked with Wong and the other men preparing for the trip. Tom listened closely, but he understood only a few words of the swift conversation. Sigh was quicker than he at learning foreign tongues.

Two of the travelers rode the horse as they filed away south along the Snake. Each man carried a mostly empty canvas pack-sack on his back. The group made its way around a bend of the river and was lost from view.

"How far is it to Baker City?" asked Tom.

"About seventy of your American miles. The men must go up the Snake River and then turn west along the base of the Wallowa Mountains. They will be in Baker City in less than three days. With heavy loads they will require five days to return."

"I hope a snowstorm doesn't catch them before they can return," said Tom.

Sigh swept a glance up at the high, pine-cloaked peaks of the Seven Devils Mountains and the opal dome of the clear sky. "I see no storm clouds."

"In mountain country, storms can come upon you with little notice."

"Yes. That is so. I have seen it happen in the California land."

Tom and Sigh turned with unspoken accord and walked to the river to begin work.

The deer in the valley of the Snake were plentiful, and unused to man, quite tame. Tom hunted them each morning during the twilight hours. He would lie in ambush with his pistol as the deer in their daily ritual left the river and climbed the mountainside to a vantage lookout point to rest the sunlit hours away. In ten days he had killed an even dozen of the animals.

On that tenth day, he worked for the first time with Yutang, hauling stones from the bar. The big Chinaman had laughed in his deep bass voice when Tom had approached at the start of the work day and took up the opposite ends of the poles of the sling. This skinny, young white man could not lift such heavy loads as Yutang was used to carrying. And if he could, surely he could not carry but a few.

Tom finished the day soaked with sweat, staggering under the weight of a large stone. At a signal from Yutang they dumped it from the sling into the water with a great splash.

Tom remained standing in the current of the river to his knees, letting it cool his hot body. Yutang laughed his rough laugh and half-bowed to the leanly sinewed white youth, acknowledging the praiseworthy accomplishment of the day's work. None of the other men had ever endured a full day as his partner on the sling.

Tom grinned, and feeling awkward in the unpracticed gesture, bowed low in acceptance of Yutang's salute. Tom liked the big man immensely. It was glorious to be alive and strong and spend a hard day with a man equally strong.

Yutang cleansed himself and walked up the hill to the cabins. Tom bathed more leisurely, gazing out over the land, enjoying the night slowly rising like blue-gray water in the far-deep hollows.

In the growing darkness, he hung his freshly washed clothing over a shoulder and, nude, went toward the light of Hoy's cooking fire shining pale yellow in the open door of the cook shack. Dry clothing would feel very fine.

From the shadows beside the wall of the cabin, Scom eyed Tom in a sly and watchful way. As Tom passed on by, he wondered why the man hated him so much. He believed that one day he might have to fight the Chinaman.

The men returned from Baker City in the afternoon of the eleventh day after their departure. They carried amazingly heavy loads upon their backs. Tom's black horse had been fitted with a much worn packsaddle and on this was tied a mount of bags and boxes of provisions.

After the supplies had been stored, Sigh declared a holiday. All the men who had stayed behind to work the claim gathered to listen to the news the travelers had heard while in Baker City.

Tom listened intently and comprehended a smattering of the talk. Sigh turned now and then and in English told him some special bits of information.

The conversation wound down and a discussion of the cost of the supplies began. Suddenly Sigh's voice rose, sharp and wrathful. He sprang up and with his fist clenched, rushed to stand over Wong.

Sigh spoke swiftly to Wong, a staccato crackling of Chinese so swift Tom caught not a word. Sigh drew back his fist as if to strike the man.

Yutang took hold of Sigh. Calmly he began to talk to the angry man. Sigh pulled away and whirling about, went outside.

He soon returned and began to talk to Wong in a tightly controlled voice. After questioning Wong and listening to the much chastened man's answers, Sigh faced Tom. "Wong bought many things at the general store in Baker City. He did not have enough fine gold dust to pay for all of it. He had with him gold nuggets that were to be left for safekeeping with Sing Chong, one of our countrymen who has a strong iron vault in his pharmacy in Baker. Wong brought out the pouch of nuggets, and there in the store in plain view of several white men, finished making payment with gold nuggets."

"Is there something wrong with that?" asked Tom.

Sigh looked out over the river for a time. Tom thought the man was not going to answer.

Then Sigh said in a flat tone, "Chinamen cannot own property in Oregon. Also they are taxed heavily for digging gold, four American dollars each three months. That is the law in Oregon. White men are jealous of us. They want us to search for gold only on old diggings that have already been worked. In these places very fine dust is all that is usually found. Only rarely a nugget. Wong showed a large pouch of nuggets to men who understand gold mining and now know we have a rich mine. Soon white men will come and take this rich claim. I feel it here." Sigh touched his heart.

"But that is not right. You told me you and the others bought the claim and have a bill of sale. Surely you are mistaken."

Sigh shrugged his shoulders. "We bought the claim. That is correct. That means something to men who are fair. To most that will not mean a thing. We will soon know if Wong has been followed. There is nothing we can do now." He looked intently at Tom and seemed about to say something. Then he walked off without further words.

Wong left also, humiliated for the major error he had committed. He may have done great harm to his comrades. Now he would suffer much *mien tzu,* loss of face. He went alone into the rocks and brush along the river. If the white men did come and take the gold, then he would kill himself.

The other men sat motionless and silent on the ground near the cabins and looked down at the rich gravel bar. The blackness of the night arrived and still they did not stir.

Tom sat among them. A nippy wind with teeth began to drone up the river valley. A star lost its moorings in the sky and fell, streaking to the north where it disappeared in a final winking flash.

Tom finally arose and walked to his pallet in the cabin and lay down. There was no worry. White men would not come to steal the gold. He went to sleep, the only man in the cabin.

Keggler angled his telescope and methodically walked the field of magnification over the shadowy forms of the Chinamen working on the gravel bar.

"There's nineteen of the heathen," he said to his men.

"Doesn't make any difference if there's a hundred of them," said Cardone, his second in command. "These Chinaboys won't fight white men. They only fight among themselves."

Keggler and his band of six men had been lying in hiding and spying upon the foreign miners since the coming of the first morning twilight. Now as he waited and watched, the sun crested the high crown of Triangle Mountain and filled all the valley with bright light. A fine light for shooting Chinamen.

Two deep valleys joined at this location. The swift Imnaha River came in from the south to merge with the much larger Snake River. The mouth of the Imnaha was choked with a fan-shaped gravel bar of three acres or so. The high water of the flood stage of the Snake in the spring dammed the smaller Imnaha, slowing its tumbling descent and causing it to drop its load of rock debris scoured from the granite flanks of the Wallowa Mountains.

"Look how fast those fellows work," said Cardone. "They act like the sun will not rise tomorrow."

"They have to work like hell," responded Keggler. "White men have already mined this bar. It was a rich one from what I have heard with many thousands of dollars of gold washed from it. The white man gave up on it last fall when the take got too thin. These Chinaboys started early this past spring. They're a patient, careful lot. They'll still make a lot of money by reworking and sifting shoveful by shovelful the whole bar once again. They'll find every speck of gold dust that was missed the first time."

"Yeh. They've probably washed out hundreds of ounces," said Canfield, a third member of the gang. "We'll get a whole summer's sluice of gold for just ten minutes' work."

Keggler made one last cautious sweep with his telescope. The men near the river seemed oblivious of anything beyond the bar. Their camp of four canvas tents was on the west side of the Snake below its junction with the Imnaha. It appeared deserted.

"Time to rob the Chinamen of their gold," said Keggler. "We'll do this same as all the other times. Canfield, LeRue, you check the tents first thing. Hustle anyone you find there down to the river. Ottoson, Vaughn, McMillan, stop your horses where your guns can cover all the gravel bar and the men there. Cardone and me will brace the Chinaboys and then make a search for their hid gold. Kill any man that tries to put up a fight."

They crawled back from the top of the brush-covered knob situated upstream on the Imnaha and went to their horses. All swung astride, and with Keggler leading, rode boldly into sight and in the direction of the miners.

One of the Chinamen spotted the string of horsemen coming along the bank of the Imnaha. He called out his discovery to his comrades. Keggler raised a hand high above his head and shouted out a greeting when he noted he had been seen by the miners. A friendly hello always put these foreigners off guard.

The miners on the bar stopped working and curiously waited for the strangers to draw near. Visitors were rare. These came from the direction of Baker City and the news they might carry would be welcome.

Keggler's cunning eyes ran over the men. They almost never owned rifles, but sometimes had pistols. He saw not one gun among them.

"All right, Canfield, LeRue, break off here and go to the camp." Keggler spoke over his shoulder to the men.

The outlaw chief raised his voice and called out to the Chinamen. "We're looking for some horses that strayed away from our diggings up on the Imnaha. Have you seen two roan horses?"

He received no answer. Had not expected one.

The bandit gang reached the edge of the gravel bar. "Ottoson, and you two other men, stop here," directed Keggler in a low voice.

The miners had left their work and drawn forward to meet the strangers. Two men moved out in front of the group.

"Those will be the ones that can talk American," said Keggler. "Now, Cardone, let's just pull our six-guns and get down to business."

Both outlaws swiftly drew their pistols.

A cry of alarm burst from the startled Chinamen. One of the men in the rear of the crowd spun around and dashed back across the bar toward a dense stand of cottonwoods.

"Cardone, shoot that fellow," ordered Keggler.

Cardone fired his revolver. The Chinaman fell. Instantly he

was up, holding his shoulder. He broke into a staggering run for the copse of trees. Cardone's pistol roared again, knocking the man down.

The wounded miner fought to his feet. Weakly, slowly, leaning so far forward he seemed ready to topple onto his face, the man continued his flight.

"Damn fine shooting," declared Keggler. "You broke both his shoulders and still left him walking. One day you may be as good as I am. Now finish it off for we've work to do."

"A head shot," said Cardone. He aimed along the short barrel of his weapon. At the sound of the cartridge exploding, the miner was slammed face down on the rocks.

"These tough little heathen make mighty fine target practice," said Cardone.

The remainder of the miners stood stock still. Keggler smelled their hatred and fear. He grinned wickedly at them.

"No one here at the camp," shouted Canfield.

"All right, come down here and help us search these Chinaboys," replied Keggler.

"Strip, you damn heathens," ordered Keggler. "Take off all your clothes. Hurry up about it." He pointed his six-gun at one of the front men. "You tell them or you are a dead man."

The miner turned and spoke quickly to the other men. Then he pulled his blouse over his head and let it drop to the ground. He slid out of his trousers and stood naked except for a belt holding a thin knife in a sheath.

"Well, well, wearing a little meat cutter," said Keggler. "Just toss it there with your clothes."

Canfield and LeRue arrived. Canfield said, "I found four pistols in the tents. Old ones that probably wouldn't work very good. That may be all the guns they have."

"Maybe so," said Keggler. "You two finish searching these monkeys and take what gold they got on them. I'll go and look for the main stash of gold."

Keggler darted a glance in one tent after another until he found the small religious shrine. He went straight to the highly polished wooden altar and brushed to the floor the offering of wine and apples in a woven basket and incense sticks in a porcelain vase. He kicked the altar aside.

Five leather pouches heavy with gold lay in a neat row on the earthen floor. Keggler smiled. The shrine might dissuade Chinamen from stealing, but to him it only meant the most likely spot to find their treasure.

Still he thoroughly ransacked all the tents for another cache. He found one golden nugget of about an ounce hidden in a roll of somebody's personal clothing. So they have thieves among their own kind, thought Keggler.

He went outside and called to his cohorts. "I believe I have found all the gold."

"Should we kill them Chinaboys and burn the camp?" asked Cardone.

CHAPTER 8

Keggler surveyed the hating faces of the miners. Then he looked over the gravel bar. Much of it had not yet been mined the second time around. A colossal joke came to him. Let the moon-eyed Celestials mine the gold. Next summer he would return and once again rob them of all their golden treasure.

He spoke to his men. "No. Let them live. Give them back all their guns and knives and let's get out of here before some white man sees us."

"Why give back the weapons?" asked Cardone.

"Why? Because we don't want someone to rob them," laughed Keggler.

The outlaw chief stowed three bags of the gold in his saddle-bags and gave two to Cardone to carry. All seven robbers swung astride and left at a gallop up the Imnaha.

Once out of sight of the Chinamen's camp, Keggler guided right, and spurring his horse, started the precipitous climb out of the valley of the Snake. His men followed, knowing the chief wanted the gang to be far away and in the company of honest men when the news of the robbery broke.

After six miles of steep climbing, the gang reached Buckhorn Spring on the high tableland. The men halted the lathered and hard-blowing horses and allowed them to drink lightly at the cold water.

"That's the meanest and roughest country God ever made," said Cardone, gazing backward at the eroded and broken land that plunged downward thousands upon thousands of feet to where the Snake and Imnaha Rivers were mere trickles of water in the bottom of the stupendous chasms.

"Rough country all right," said Canfield. "But there's one thing about it I like."

"What's that?" questioned Cardone.

"There's hundreds of Chinaboys down there working like slaves to dig gold for us."

All the men laughed.

Keggler led off, holding west of the breaks of the Imnaha. The route traversed gently rolling forested country sloping at a low angle to the south. The cayuses traveled easily on the mat of needles beneath the tall pine trees.

In late afternoon they came out of the timber and crossed the flat valley of the Wallowa River. By the time darkness overran the gang, they had climbed into the Wallowa Mountains to Moccasin Spring Lake lying under the crown of Glacier Mountain.

There was snow in the shade of the trees and a cold wind blew down from the glacier on the mountaintop. The band found a dry spot and made camp. The horses were staked out to graze the dry alpine grass.

"If I'd known we were going to be in snow, I'd have brought another blanket," complained LeRue.

"You can stand one cold night," said Keggler. "We'll be in Baker City well before dark tomorrow."

The gang moved fast the following day, trotting their horses where the land allowed it. At noon they crossed the Powder River and two hours later drew near Baker City, lying under Elkhorn Peak of the Blue Mountains.

Weeks before when they had first arrived in the territory, the robbers had rented a house on the outskirts of the town. Now they rode in at a leisurely pace so as not to draw attention to themselves. They stopped at the house and stabled the horses.

"Spread out and drift around and let people see you," directed Keggler. "No one will believe we robbed those Chinamen yesterday far away on the Snake River."

Keggler placed a nickle on the top of the counter of Thompson's General Store and helped himself to a handful of hard candy from a large glass container. As he sucked on one of the sweets, he idly watched Thompson and his Chinese clerk dealing with a group of Chinese miners.

The miners had arrived at the store a few steps ahead of Keggler, ten small brown men with two of them riding a long-legged black horse. An excellent mount, judged Keggler and he wondered how the Chinamen had gained possession of him.

The leader of the group of miners called out in the Chinese language the names of various items from a list. The clerk interpreted for Thompson who moved about the long aisles of the store collecting the desired provisions. The store owner in turn sounded the price to the clerk. With nimble fingers, the man tallied the cost with a flick of wooden balls on an abacus board.

Finally the list was exhausted and the clerk told the total cost. He set a scale on the counter and placed a brass weight in one of the pans hanging on the delicate balance arm.

"It will require gold sufficient to equal the brass piece four times to pay for all you have purchased," the clerk told the miner. "Supplies are very expensive because they must be shipped from San Francisco."

The man nodded his understanding and handed a bag of gold dust to the clerk.

The pan was filled three times. The gold pouch became empty before the balancing bar was in equilibrium for the fourth time.

"About two more ounces of gold are needed," the clerk told the miner.

The man reached inside his blouse and extracted a second pouch. He untied the neck and poured a mound of nuggets into his palm. He selected a nugget he judged to be approximately the correct weight and added it to the higher pan of the scale.

"Close to being in balance," said the clerk. "You have four dollars coming in change."

At the appearance of the nugget on the scale, Keggler sidled a couple of steps to the side so he could better see the quantity of gold the miner held. He was astounded at the pile of nuggets in the Chinaman's hand and the large bulk of the pouch that obviously contained many more. Somewhere these foreigners had struck a rich deposit.

Keggler strode across the store toward the outside. The comrades of the miners making the purchases stood and waited in a group by the door. Before they could get out of Keggler's way, he roughly elbowed a passageway through them.

Once in the street, the robber chief quickened his step. The members of his band must be gathered, for there was much nugget gold to steal. And nuggets always brought a large premium over dust.

Many nuggets meant the heathen were mining virgin ground. If that was indeed true, Keggler would do more than steal what gold they had washed out in their sluice boxes. He would take the whole claim, for he had always wanted to own a rich gold mine. Even if that could only be accomplished by killing most of the Chinamen in the state of Oregon.

Tom awoke in the morning after Wong's return from Baker City to a shuffle of feet on the earthen floor. Sigh was at a table near the door. A sheet of paper and writing brush and ink were in front of him.

Several men were lined up and passing before him. As they did so, each took up the brush and signed the piece of paper.

"What is going on?" asked Tom.

"We are giving our gold claim to you," said Sigh. "Then we will work for wages."

"I don't want your gold," said Tom, rising quickly.

"Then if there is no trouble with white men from Baker City, you can return the claim to us," replied Sigh.

"I will surely do that," said Tom. "But I don't believe there will be any problem with Americans wanting your claim."

There was a scuffle at the doorway and a series of shrill Chinese curses. Scom came sprawling inside. Yutang followed immediately and caught him by the queue and arm and lifted him erect.

"Sign the paper," Yutang ordered. "Do it now or I will break your stubborn neck."

Scom grabbed up the brush and make his mark with savage strokes. "This white man now owns our gold. We will never get it back."

"Scom, there are times when we must trust one of the white men," said Sigh. "I believe Tom is the one."

"I think otherwise. You are a fool." Scom spun to look at all the men. "All of you are fools."

"We shall find out," said Sigh. He folded the paper that transferred the ownership of the claim and offered it to Tom.

"Keep it for now," Tom told Sigh. He turned away and, uneasy about the whole chain of events, went outside.

The day was gray and an ill-tempered wind gusted under a lowering sky. A thick mass of clouds clung to the flanks of Seven Devils Mountains like a shroud. A trickle of snowflakes glided down.

The fisherman waited with his basket. He bowed slightly to Tom. "Good morning," he said.

"Good morning, Mook," replied Tom and returned the greeting bow.

Without further conversation, they left together, heading downriver. The fisherman had seen several deer bedding in a large patch of brush near his fish traps. He had informed Tom of his discovery and they had agreed upon a hunt in the early morning before the deer were disturbed by the presence of Mook emptying the fish traps of the night's catch.

On the gravel bar, Sigh placed the golden cube on its stone pedestal and the men began their labor. The pace was sluggish. As the morning wore away, the men often glanced up the river channel along the trail from Baker City.

"Sigh, they come as you said they would," said Yutang, stabbing a hand to the south.

Sigh pivoted to stare and counted six horsemen winding their course beside the Snake. He felt a cold chill. Would his scheme of giving the gold-filled gravel bar to Tom stop these men from taking it? Or had he merely placed his young friend in a very hazardous position? Would Tom be sacrificed and the gold still lost to the strangers?

"I see Tom returning far down the river," said Sigh. "Go and get the bill of sale and give it to him. Bring him here as fast as you can."

Yutang sped up the slope to the cabin. A moment later he came outside and ran down the river.

Keggler led his gang of five around the last curve of the river and approached the cabins. He swiftly estimated the number of men who had stopped working and watched the horsemen from the long gravel bar.

Keggler spoke to his cohorts. "There's a big bunch of those Chinaboys. I wish LeRue was here, for we may have need for one more gun. Canfield, you work alone. Check the cabins quick and come stand with us. Ottoson, Vaughn, McMillan, get your rifles ready. Shoot the damn heathen if they give us the least bit of trouble. I mean to have the gold they've dug and their claim, too, if it is as rich as those nuggets showed it might be."

Cardone loosened his six-gun in its holster. "Keggler, I sure wouldn't mind some target practice shooting some of those moon-eyed Celestials."

"You just might get the chance. You watch whoever acts like he is boss. Kill him quick if he starts to signal the others to jump us."

Keggler guided the way past the cabins and angled down toward the river. Just above the gravel bar, he motioned a halt.

"Ottoson, you three stop here and keep on guard. Cardone, come with me. Watch like I told you to."

"We can take them easy," said Cardone.

On the bar, Keggler and Cardone dismounted. Casually they scanned the brown faces of the Chinamen who stood uneasily looking at them.

"Just as I suspicioned, only heathen here," said Keggler.

Ignoring Sigh and the other Chinese, Keggler walked to the nearest sluice box and with his knife began to sort through the material trapped in the bottom. He found a nugget the size of a pea.

He chortled loudly and held the golden kernel up for Cardone to see. Then he roved his sight over the bar.

"This is virgin ground. And damn rich from what I can see. They can't claim this property. Whatever is here is ours for the taking. Now, Chinaboys, what is that on top of that rock there in the center of the bar?"

Keggler strode to the mound of rock that had been left behind as all the remainder of the bar on all sides was worked lower and lower.

"Good God!" exclaimed Keggler. "Cardone, there's a chunk of gold laying here half as big as your fist. We are rich."

"The claim owner will not like for you to take his gold," said Sigh, coming up to Keggler.

"What's that you say? What owner? I don't see anyone here but you coolie fellows, and you can't own horse manure let alone gold-bearing land."

"The owner comes now. There on the side of the river." Sigh pointed.

Keggler ranged his view along the river. A tall, lanky white man and a heavy-set Chinaboy were hurrying up the Snake.

"There may be a little trouble, Cardone. I wasn't counting on an American being here. Still, this claim looks to be one damn fine patch of ground. Let's play it out a little farther and see what happens."

"I see only one man," replied Cardone. "He'll be easy to kill. These Chinaboys won't help him and they can't testify in a court of law against white men regardless what they see."

Tom slowed and raked his eyes over the six armed white men. Three were sitting their horses on the slope above the bar. Their rifles were out of the scabbards and resting across the saddle in front of them. Another man came out of one of the cabins, mounted and rode to join them. Two more of the strangers were in the center of the bar. Both wore pistols. One held the golden cube in his gun hand.

Sigh stood five or six paces behind the white man with the cube. The other Chinamen were scattered over the bar.

Tom angled a course to come up on the right side of the line of four mounted men. Their rifles were pointing to the left away from him. The nearest horseman blocked the view of his comrades. Only this one man was in a position to make a fast shift to bring his rifle to bear on Tom.

Yutang walked out on the gravel bar to stand beside Sigh and near Keggler and Cardone. The big Chinaman regarded Tom closely. How much courage did the white youth possess?

"What can I do for you fellows?" Tom asked.

Keggler evaluated the young man before him. He had a sparse stubble of beard. His black shoulder-length hair was pulled back behind his head and tied with a strip of blue cotton cloth. He was dressed in blue pants and blouse like those the Chinamen wore. The outfit was much too small for him. The holster and pistol belted over the Chinaman clothing looked outlandish.

"This fellow 'pears to be turning into a Chinee heathen like all of the rest of them here," Keggler said to his men and began to laugh.

A few of the other white men snickered at the comment. Keggler nonchalantly changed the golden cube to his left hand.

Tom felt the hot blood rush to his head. Then he squashed the anger. Never let an enemy make you mad—he could hear the voice giving the advice rush up out of his memories.

"This Chinaboy says you are the owner of this claim," Keggler said to Tom. "Let me see your recorded claim notice or a bill of sale."

Tom reached inside his blouse and extracted the paper Yutang had given him. He held it in his left hand and idly waved it in the air a couple of times. He knew it was worthless. The Chinamen could not own property, so therefore, they surely could not sign it over to him. However, he would never tell them that.

"Let me see it," said Keggler.

"I don't have to show you anything," retorted Tom in a flinty voice. "You are trespassing on private property. Take your friends and move on."

The sharpness of the response surprised Keggler.

The big smile on his face washed away. He growled at Tom, "You are mighty rough talking with six of us here. Just show me your ownership papers for these diggings and we'll leave."

"I was here first, so this ground belongs to me," said Tom. "That is the law. And if I want to work these men, that is my business. Now get off my property." Tom put the paper in his shirt. He knew that the showing of a document, no matter how valid, would not stop what was going to happen here.

"Keggler, let me take care of this," snarled Cardone. His face had grown hard and a merciless glitter was in his eyes.

"Then do it," snapped Keggler.

Cardone moved two paces nearer Tom. "You are just a smart-aleck kid with a gun," said Cardone. He set himself to draw his six-gun. "Even if you have recorded a gold claim, you're not old enough to hold it under the law. Now don't try to play men's games. Take your heathen Chinaboys and clear out."

Tom felt the wolf rise in his heart at the ruthless disregard for the rights of the Chinamen and his own. He knew the battle was now.

Cardone had expected the youth to show doubt, perhaps fear at the challenge. Instead he saw the youth's eyes measuring the position of his opponents, plotting the strategy for the fight. Cardone had seen skilled gunmen make such surveys, had made them himself. Strange to see one so young act so professionally. A momentary doubt of how the gunplay might end touched Cardone.

He shrugged it off, confident of the swiftness of his hand.

CHAPTER 9

Tom looked at Sigh and saw in the man's taut and nervous face that he would not fight the intruders. Tom darted a glance at Yutang. He was the only other man close enough to the two white men to launch an attack upon them.

Yutang's sight met his and read the probing query. He showed his teeth in a slit of a grin and half closed an eye for an instant.

Tom saw the big Chinaman's black eye close and open and the watchfulness and calculation and a light of battle come into his countenance.

A hot flame of elation touched Tom. With Yutang's help, he just might live through this fight.

"Take your coolies and get out while you are still alive," roared Cardone.

The battle might as well start now, thought Tom. "To hell with you!" He threw the challenge back in a tight and icy voice. "You get off this property."

"Keggler, kill the bastards," yelled Cardone and swiftly drew his six-gun.

Tom pulled his pistol from its holster with a flick of his wrist. The .45-caliber weapon bucked in his hand.

Cardone was flung backward. A startled expression suddenly contorted his face.

Keggler leaned forward toward Tom and began the draw of his revolver. Stunned by seeing Cardone fall, Keggler knew he was late in his action. He should not have sent Cardone to kill the kid. He should have done it himself.

Yutang screamed a savage, guttural cry. He leapt in the direction of the outlaw chief, his stout body moving with unnatural speed and formidable strength.

Seeing Yutang springing at the second white man, Tom whirled left toward the nearest rider. The man was swinging his rifle around. He had a very long distance to turn to shoot down at Tom.

Too far and too slow. Tom's bullet drove in under the rifleman's ribs, continuing up at a slant, plowing through the soft lungs and breaking the thick bone of the clavicle as it tore free of the body at the top of the shoulder.

The man tumbled sideways from the saddle and struck hard upon the ground. His horse, frightened by the explosion of Tom's gun so close, lunged left to escape. It stepped upon the corpse and slammed into the next rifleman's steed, nearly upsetting it.

Yutang crashed into Keggler from behind before he could shoot. The Chinaman's arm encircled the outlaw's chest and hoisted him up from the ground. At the same moment he ripped the half-drawn pistol from Keggler's hand and hurled the weapon away.

Yutang locked a hold in Keggler's hair and wrenched the man's head far to the rear. He stopped just short of breaking the spinal column.

"Tell the foreign devils I will snap their leader's neck if they hurt Tom," Yutang yelled at Sigh.

"Stop! Stop the shooting or this man is dead!" Sigh cried out loudly in English.

Keggler arched backward to relieve some of the pressure on his neck and twisted to break free. He was a child in Yutang's hands. The Chinaman held him firmly and applied more force, feeling the vertebrae grinding upon each other.

Keggler shrieked in horrible pain, the pitch mounting to a keening intensity that was not human. His arms fluttered and he went limp.

"Hold your fire," bellowed Ottoson. "That damn Chinaman's got Keggler in a death grip. Look's like his neck's already 'bout broke off."

Tom backed away to where he had a clear line of sight at the three remaining riflemen. He called out, "Sigh, take their guns. Don't get between them and me. Hurry it. Now move."

Sigh sped up to the first rider and held out his hand for the man's weapons. The man gripped his rifle and looked uncertainly from Yutang to Keggler.

"All of you give your rifles and six-guns and all your ammunition to Sigh," Tom ordered. "Yutang will sure as hell kill that man if you don't."

As the riders still hesitated, Tom raised his pistol. "Give your guns to Sigh," he shouted out in a strident voice. He must get the firearms now or quickly start the battle anew before they all attacked him in unison.

"What will you do if we give them up?" asked Ottoson.

"You can go on your way safely," replied Tom. "All we want is to be left alone."

"All right," agreed Ottoson. He called out to the other outlaws, "Give the damn Chinaman your guns."

All three gave their rifles and pistols to Sigh. He backed away with his armload of weapons and cartridge belts to stand beside Tom.

"Yutang, let the man go," Tom said.

"No. Now I finish tearing off his head," replied Yutang in a vengeful tone.

"We have their guns," said Tom. "They can't harm us."

"It is stupid to let our enemies live. They can get more guns in Baker City and return. We must kill them now that we have the chance. I can do it so very easily. Just a little jerk."

Sigh spoke to Yutang. "Tom is correct. We said they could go safely away from here. Let them know we are men who honor our word."

"Honor can get a man killed," said Yutang. He wrestled with his doubts about releasing the outlaw leader. With misgivings, he said, "You two are my friends so I will do what you ask."

Yutang threw Keggler away from him as if he were something rotten. The outlaw fell upon the rocks.

"Help him to get on his horse," Tom motioned for Ottoson to go down to the river bar.

Ottoson guided his mount up beside Keggler's steed, caught the reins and led the animal to the man lying on the ground. "He can't set up, let alone ride," Ottoson said.

"If he can't ride, then tie him on," ordered Tom. He jerked a thumb at the other two outlaws. "You two get down there and put him up on his horse."

The men lifted Keggler astride. He teetered in the saddle and would have fallen had Ottoson not steadied him.

"Rope his feet under the horse's belly," commanded Ottoson.

The men quickly complied and remounted. At Ottoson's signal, the bandits walked their mustangs up from the river and once on the level ground, kicked them into a trot south on the trail to Baker City.

"I know we should have killed them," Yutang said. "We will regret the day we let them leave here alive."

"We have guns now," said Tom. "They will not attack knowing that."

Sigh shook his head. "In China only soldiers and Triad warriors have firearms. Very few of us who were farmers have ever fired a gun. And even we who have used them are very poor at hitting a target."

Tom pointed up at the cold, heavy overcast and the white flakes in the air. "Winter has arrived. The mountains and a deep snow should stop anyone from bothering us until spring."

"The bar is about one-third searched for gold," said Sigh. "If we work as fast as we can during the winter, we can have about half the gold washed by the time spring comes. Another full year will be needed to completely sluice all the gravel and many things can happen in that span of time."

"During the winter, I will teach you to shoot. We can then post guards on lookout next summer and be safe."

"A better plan would have been to kill all of them so they could not return," Yutang said.

"Let's get some tools and bury these two dead men," said Tom.

"No burial for these thieves," growled Yutang. "Their flesh should be eaten by worms and their bones scattered widely over the land."

"Even thieves deserve a Christian burial," argued Tom.

"You have saved us from our enemies, Tom, and I want to do what you ask," Yutang said. "But these men could not be Christians, and I am not Christian. They are bandits and deserve to go into the river."

Yutang went to the slain rifleman on the slope. Catching the man by the foot, Yutang dragged the body unceremoniously over the rocks to Cardone. Hesitating a second to take hold of the gunman's collar, the Chinaman towed both corpses out into the swift water of the Snake.

Blood swirled away from the bodies and soiled the water as Yutang gave the corpses to the current. They floated for three or four yards and then as their clothing became soaked, sank into the watery depths.

"All of you give the miserable dogs your worst curses," Yutang called to the crowd of men standing and watching from the shore.

A chorus of Chinese invectives rang out over the turbulent flow of the Snake River. Only Tom said not a word.

During the night, the snowstorm fell upon the valley of the Snake like a mean white dog. Throughout the black hours, a frigid wind hummed through the cracks in the walls of the ill-built cabin. Tom rolled himself in his thin coverlet and wished for another to ward off the chill.

Dawn light crept in slowly. The Chinamen arose, but did not go out to work. They merely gazed out into the storm and then congregated in groups and talked or played games of cards.

Tom took one of the rifles and went out into the storm. The deer would be driven down from the high mountain slopes by the snow and would gather in the brushy areas adjacent to the river. The wolves, the predatory nemesis of the deer, would also come there to feed upon them. Their prime winter pelts would make an excellent sleeping robe.

Tom built a blind of broken juniper limbs on the downwind edge of a field of bitterbrush. The deer would come to the dark green bush, their favorite winter food.

He waited, the snow mounding around him. Then the deer came, scores of bucks with antlers held high, does, yearling and fawns of the past spring, down the ancient game trails through the pine forest. Warily they stole into the bitterbrush, sniffing the wind, listening, watching.

The deer did not detect Tom sitting motionless behind his ring of obscuring juniper. They scattered, wandering among the clumps of brush to feed on the leaves and tender tips of the branches.

The hours passed. The storm piled the snow to a depth of a foot or more.

Silently as the fall of the snowflakes, five grayish-black wolves ghosted in, coming up the wind off on Tom's left. He raised his rifle and waited for their closest point of approach.

They halted. Tom sighted on the large male on the far side of the pack. Always shoot the most distant one first.

The rifle cracked and the wolf was slammed down. In startled confusion the animals hesitated. Tom killed a second.

Then the remaining three wolves were in a flat-out streaking run. Tom caught one in his sights, tracked it for a second and burst its heart with a lead projectile. It collapsed, tumbling end over end in a flurry of snow.

The deer panicked, bounding away in all directions.

Tom went to the slain wolves. The fur, after a proper tanning, and softening by gently pounding between two stones, would make a soft sleeping robe, one that would keep him warm to many degrees below zero.

In the evening, Tom rested on his pallet and let his mind wander. For many days he had been busy with hunting, toiling on the bar from daylight to dark, and sleeping so deeply as to be almost unconscious. He was surprised at how easily he had settled into the ritual of the Chinamen. Not once had he considered leaving. Scom's threatening demeanor bothered him at times, but now since the fight with the white outlaws, all the other men had accepted him and he was comfortable in their companionship.

He felt the slow gathering-in of his memories, time falling away, going back to his deepest recollections. Back past the sheriff's posse, the killings in Westfall and out to the mountain made of lava in the center of the Alvord Desert. He recalled the glacial man who never smiled. His father, who had reared him in that land without other humans.

He had no memories of his mother. His inquiries to his father about her drew only one response: "Women are very desirable, but completely unpredictable."

Tom was not entirely certain what the full meaning of the comment was. He felt the bittersweat emotion of sorrow for not having known the woman that had mothered him.

For twelve years Tom and his father lived alone in the desert. Often his father was gone for days and weeks. In those times the boy had survived by his own strength and skill.

He roamed the mountains and far out on the desert. He tracked the deer, mountain lion and wolf, following the sign for many miles. He stalked the big predators as they stalked their own prey. Only rarely did he kill one of them. Always at the end of these excursions, he hurried home to the small stone house and the single spring on the mountain, hoping his father had returned in his absence.

The man would return with gold and paper money and packhorses laden with provisions. Every time he brought a box of books. The man and boy would talk and the lessons would begin again—the many lessons of reading, arithmetic, history, and geography. One lesson was practiced every day: the use of firearms.

Tom could hear the sound of his father's voice giving instructions. It had a flat tone, an emotionless timbre that never varied regardless of whether he was correcting Tom's arithmetic or telling him where to shoot a man to kill him most swiftly.

In the years of growing up in that harsh desert land, the months alternated between complete freedom when his father was not present and intensive training when the man was there. Until Tom began to continue the lessons in the absence of his father. And the day when he saw the picture of a fine stone house in a book.

Tom questioned his father how such a structure could be built. The man sketched out, in a beautifully accurate hand, a plan for the construction of the house.

Tom launched himself into the task of building with flat slabs of lava and mortar of mud. He enjoyed the use of his muscles, feeling the pleasant strain of lifting the heavy stones higher than his head to lay the walls and carrying tons and tons of mud. He remembered the fabulous day, the only time his father ever gave him a compliment: "You are a strong man and your hands are quick. You are better than most men you will ever encounter."

Then in one of those rare moments when his father gave advice about how to survive in the world of men, he had continued. "Do not hurt other men, but also do not allow them to hurt you or take what is yours. There may be times when you have to kill. Do not grow to like it."

The man had lapsed into silence and had not spoken for the

remainder of the day, as if he had said something that had turned him completely inward.

The roof of the house was a problem, for there were only stunted juniper on the desert mountain, nothing long enough from which to make the ceiling joists. Though it was the mild season of autumn when the need arose for the timbers, his father had required them to wait until the bitter winter arrived before he led the way with all five horses to a distant forested mountain. Three trips were made, snaking the long pine saplings across the flower-white Alvord. They saw not one other human being. Tom thought his father had planned it that way.

The quiet man and Tom lived the last days of the cold season in the large stone house. In the early spring the man grew restless. One day he saddled and, leading an extra horse, rode away to the northeast. As was his custom, he said nothing of his destination or when he would return.

Tom continued his studies and practice with rifle and pistols. He read completely through the box of books and several other volumes for the second time before his father returned.

The big gray horse carrying his father came to the stone house in the middle of the night. Tom heard the iron-shod hooves on the rocky yard and went outside.

Gallatin lay along the neck of his mount, arms weakly clutching the long, coarse hair of the mane. Blood leaked steadily from a deep bullet wound in his chest. Tom took him down in his arms and carried him inside. Gently he placed his father on a bunk.

Gallatin's wound did not respond to Tom's simple medical treatment. Not once did the man mention obtaining the aid of a doctor. His strong body wasted away.

In those last days, Gallatin spent many hours drawing, measuring and covering a whole deer hide with characters and figures depicting the surrounding country. He would erase and modify as necessary. Sometimes resting for a day or more at a time, he would recall and add some unusual but important detail such as a wet-weather spring, a break in a rimrock that would allow a passage where no one expected, a natural cave, a secret hidden camp with water and grass and defensible from attack, or just a game trail in steep terrain that a horse could navigate.

He gave Tom knowledge accumulated and gleaned from years

of searching, always with the expectation of its use for the very safety of his life. He ransacked every nook and cranny of his memory and recorded the great storehouse of facts to help a son survive until he also knew intimately every canyon, spring, and hidden trail.

Then all the information was condensed and inscribed on a perfect piece of tanned deer hide. The distance scale was exact with the house on the mountain in the center. No legend existed to interpret the map; he and Tom had designed their own symbols, and thus the chart was almost useless to another man.

Gallatin died in the middle of the summer when the land lay tortured beneath the desert sun. Tom buried his father under a tall mound of black lava rock.

Tom spent many hours studying and admiring his inheritance, not just as a map, but for its symmetry, style and form. Without knowing what art was, he knew his father had created something very beautiful. And just for him.

Tom had clung to the map, for he had so little information to guide and protect him in his travel through the world of men. However, now he also had friends. His father had never told him of the warm, happy feeling that existed when one was with people he liked. Perhaps his father never had a friend. Tom felt sad at that possibility.

In the afternoon of the second day of the storm, a ghost disk of a sun shone through the thinning clouds. The men put on coats and went out into the foot of snow and down to the river bar. In the deep cold, the men's breath showed as a cloud as they skimmed the snow away and fell into their routine of swift and silent assault upon the deposit of gravel and rock.

The men labored late, for the white snow seemed to have a luminescent glow all its own to brighten the dusk of evening. When they finally gathered in the cabin and the day's washing of gold was spread on a plate for viewing, the men said not a word. Each wondered silently if the white men of this foreign land would let them leave with any wealth at all.

CHAPTER 10

Weeks meandered into deep winter. Some days the weather was good enough to allow the men to work outside. In those periods the men hurried at their tasks of shoveling and sifting large amounts of sand and gravel for its gold.

During the long, cold evenings when the snow fell, Tom and Sigh taught each other their language before the fireshine. The other Chinamen talked among themselves in low voices like strange sundown birds before they fell silent at last and the only sound was the wind outside and Tom and Sigh murmuring awkward, foreign words.

Sometimes with the language lessons done and the Chinamen asleep, Tom sat for a long time without moving a muscle, without blinking, speculating upon the nature of his unpleasant deeds, the killing of other men. Then he would consider and reflect upon what different action he could have taken. Each time he could think of nothing else he could have done without letting his enemies harm him or his friends. His father had told him never to let that happen.

Tom ceased his moralizing and found real peace with the Chinamen. The peace of hard work with men who knew nothing except hard work. And the peace of resting quietly with them afterwards, in the late hours when the day became black. Then, heavy-lidded with weariness, Tom would crawl into his blankets on the pallet of straw and sleep in the dark of the midnight cabin deep in the valley beside the Snake.

The day was clear. Thick ice, like polished steel, lined the banks of the Snake River. A frigid wind came down from the snowy mountains, eating away the warmth of the bodies of the men laboring on the gravel bar.

No use could be made of the sluice boxes. The river had accumulated winter in its depth and the water taken from it turned instantly to ice upon being thrown into the riffled wooden trough. All the men concentrated on carrying the bigger stones and rolling the boulders from the bar.

Yutang, Scom, Yuen and Tom worked at the base of a large round boulder that had been deposited in the gravel bar in some ancient unrecorded age. They had dug a sloping trench from the stone to the water's edge. Now the last of the material of the foundation of the boulder was being removed. The men hoped to start the stone rolling and then its momentum would carry it down the trench and into the river.

"It is close to moving," said Yutang, climbing out of the pit. "Only a thin base holds it. Now let's use the pry poles to tip it over. All four of us put our pressure on this uphill side."

They strained on the ends of their leverage poles. The boulder swayed, then settled back into its original position.

"Its rounded form makes it difficult to apply enough force to move it without the poles slipping off," said Tom.

"I can apply much more force with my shoulder," said Yutang. "I will go down into the hole and push. All the rest of you pry."

"It is dangerous to be in the hole with the rock," cautioned Tom.

"I know. Do not let it fall back on me."

Yutang sprang into the pit behind the bounder. He grinned up at the other men. "This time we make it roll into the river. There is often much gold at the base of these big rocks. Give all your strength. Now heave!"

An edge of the stone lifted an inch, six inches, a foot up from its resting place.

Yutang's foot, thrusting powerfully, slipped as the ground crumpled beneath it. His leg went in under the boulder. At that moment Scom's pole lost its hold. The giant stone toppled back into its previous location with a loud crunching sound.

A colossal moan erupted from Yutang. He looked up at Tom, his black eyes wide pools of hurt. "Help me," he cried.

"Set your poles to pry," Tom yelled at Scom and Yuen.

He leaped into the pit beside Yutang. He placed his feet against the rear wall at waist height and his shoulders on the massive stone.

"Pry, you bastards," Tom screamed up at the two men above.

He put his strength on the rock. His mind contained but one thought—move the stone off his friend.

Sharp projections of rock stabbed into his back. His tendons and muscles creaked. His breath was compressed and locked like a solid in his lungs.

He put forth his ultimate effort. Stars exploded in his brain.

He sensed the stone shifting. Then he could no longer feel it. He fell beside Yutang.

And he heard the wonderful sound of the boulder rumbling down the trench to the river.

Men sprang into the hole and many hands lifted Yutang and Tom out. Gently they were laid on the ground.

Tom rested, breathing deeply, recovering from the tremendous effort. Yuen's voice reached him. It was a sob.

Tom rolled over to look. All the men were gathered around Yutang. The big man raised his head and gazed steadily at Tom.

"You did a mighty feat in moving that stone," said Yutang. "You are stronger than I am."

"Only because I had your strength as well as my own there for just a moment," replied Tom. "How is your foot?"

"See for yourself."

From the middle of the lower leg to the ends of the toes, Yutang's leg was horribly crushed. Shattered bones protruded from the flesh in a score of places. Blood spouted in red geysers from ruptured arteries. Yuen was working speedily to tie a tourniquet to stop the bleeding.

Tom knew with sorrow that the leg was lost. He had difficulty in keeping his voice from breaking as he spoke to Yutang.

"Many men live long lives with only one leg."

Tom was mystified at the odd expression that came onto the faces of the men hovering near Yutang. What thoughts had his words created in them.

"Scom, where are you?" called Yutang in an iron voice. "Ah, there you are. I believe you deliberately let that rock fall on me. Now don't deny it because there is nothing you can say that will change my mind."

"Then I will say nothing," growled Scom and sank back into the crowd.

"Don't anyone try to take revenge on Scom for me," said Yutang. "One day I will take him in these hands and remove his head." Yutang became silent, laying motionless. His eyes lifted upward past the sparkling snow-white peaks of Seven Devils Mountains to roam the sky. A wistful expression cloaked his broad countenance.

The other men remained still as if afraid to intrude into Yutang's private reverie.

Several minutes passed before Yutang lowered his sight from the heavens to the earth.

"Hoy, I am hungry. Bring me some of your delicious fish soup."

"Yes, Yutang. Right away," said Hoy, his face strained. He stood up.

"Hoy, one last favor. Put a black pearl in it for me. I wish to take a long journey."

"Are you very sure, Yutang?" Hoy asked, and once again stooped to be close to the injured man.

"I am certain."

"Then I will do it." With a haunted look, Hoy went up the slope to the shanties.

Tom was surprised at the turn of the conversation. Yutang wanted to eat when all attention should have been concentrated on treating his wound. And the term "black pearl" seemed to have a large significance. Was it some kind of special Chinese spice?

The men huddled ever closer to Yutang. Some reached out and touched him. When Hoy returned with the soup, the group provided a passageway for him.

Yutang ate slowly, savoring the food. He swallowed the last spoonful and looked around.

"Sit me up so the sun can shine brightly on me, for death loves a shining mark. I am ready to meet joss."

Sigh and Yuen raised Yutang and placed his back to rest against a snow-covered rock. They sat down on the ground very near him.

Yutang raised his view to the heavens and sat motionless. "Ah! Isn't the sunlight glimmering off the snowy shoulders of Seven Devils a wonderful sight?"

No one spoke or turned to look.

"I feel the dragon stirring," said Yutang. "I will soon be dead. I would thank my friends to send my bones to China to the Flowery Kingdom. I hope and think you will. Then my spirit will have peace forever."

"What is happening?" Tom whispered to Hoy.

"Yutang has taken the black pill. It is opium. I put much of it in the soup as he asked. It will soon kill him." Hoy spoke so low Tom had doubt he had heard correctly.

"But he could live with one foot. We could cut it off quickly and a strong man like him would not die."

"What would a one-legged Chinaman do here in the mountains of a foreign land? He cannot work. The rest of us do not have enough money above our own needs to clothe him. Yutang is a proud man. He would rather die than to be dishonored by begging."

"My spirit rises up from the land," said Yutang in a calm voice. "I am flying swiftly over the forested mountains and the dry desert. I see Gum San To Foy, the big city of the Golden Mountains. There below me is the shore of the great sea where we first set foot upon this country of white men. Now I am speeding swiftly over the wide, deep sea. Oh, how beautiful it is. The sky is without clouds and the same wondrous blue as the ocean."

Yutang quivered as more of the potent narcotic flooded into his blood. His drug-induced dream intensified and his speech increased in tempo and the pitch rose.

"Canton! My brothers, I can see Canton. I am approaching it very fast. I can hear the thousands of people at the marketplace and smell the wonderful odors of incense, soy and cooking oils."

Yutang's body trembled and arched as the concentration of opium reached a toxic level and seared the nerve endings. He fought for control. He spoke again.

"I am at my father's farm. He has planted cabbage in one field and rice in the other. It will be a bountiful harvest. I am finally home."

All the men listened intently and without a murmur to Yutang's recital of his vision. No one commented that it was the dead of winter in China and nothing grew in the fields. They hunkered very near him, many with their eyes closed, living his vision of home with him.

Yutang began to twitch. His eyes opened widely and the pupils dilated. His legs and arms jerked as convulsions seized his thick frame. His body beat up and down on the rocks.

Sigh and Hoy fell upon the thrashing figure, placing all their weight to hold it still. They were as chaff against the massive strength of Yutang. Yuen and Tom piled their body weights upon the mound of men.

Yutang grimaced in shock and sudden agony of death. There was a last rattle of air in his throat. His face softened and eyes steadied and came to final rest.

Sigh reached out and brushed the eyelids down to cover the black orbs. "The black pill has done its work," he said.

He stood up. "Yutang shall receive his share of gold as if he were alive. We will send it to his father. His bones shall sail back to China with me."

The stormy days of December passed drearily. Tom felt only gloom at Yutang's death and spoke little to the other men.

Snow lay two feet deep. The men remained in the cabin, venturing out only to chop more wood to feed the voracious appetite of the open fireplaces.

In the late part of the month, a dense ice fog settled into the valley and obscured the sun. For days it endured, restricting the range of sight to a few yards.

One day, late in the evening, loud shouts sounded from down the river. Sigh, Tom and the total group streamed from the shanties. Tom and five other men were armed with the rifles captured from the outlaws.

Phantom forms like spirits moved in the ice mist at the base of the mountains. Then they materialized into full view, eighteen men in a line. One man broke trail through the snow and the others followed exactly in his footsteps.

The strangers called out greetings in Chinese and were happily answered by Sigh's group.

"It is Guofeng and his comrades," said Sigh. "They have come all the long distance from their mine on the Imnaha River." He hurried forward to greet the lead man with a bear hug.

Old friends were made welcome. Some of the younger men

did a happy, wild dance in the snow with their countrymen they had not seen for months.

The new arrivals became instantly silent as Tom came nearer and was recognized as a white man.

"What is a foreign devil doing among you?" angrily questioned Guofeng.

Sigh walked to the tall American and put his hand on his shoulder. "This foreign devil saved our gold and perhaps our very lives. But come inside for you must be tired. Have hot tea and I will tell you the story."

As the newcomers sipped the strong beverage, Sigh described the incident of the thieves and Tom's and Yutang's deeds. Guofeng found the tale pleasing and asked for it to be told a second time with more detail.

"I would have given much to see the fight. I am glad you shot two of the bandits. From your description they are the very same men who killed my brother Woen and stole our gold. Sigh, you should have let Yutang break the leader's neck. All of them deserved to die. It is sad that part of them still lives."

"Tell us what happened to your gold," said Sigh.

With a sad countenance, Guofeng did as asked. Then he wiped the sorrow from his face. He said, "But now it is the New Year. A new start must be made. We have come to share this day with you. It is the time to pay honest debts, visit friends, and buy new clothes. We owe no money and cannot buy new clothes, so we will visit with our friends for a day and talk of home and women."

"You must be hungry," said Hoy. "I will prepare you some food."

"Not just food," said Sigh. "We must have a feast."

"Yes. A great feast," agreed Guofeng. "We have brought special delicacies of dried abalone and oysters shipped from California, and our cook has sprouted beans which he has carried all the way on his back."

Hoy clapped his hands gleefully. "Give them to me and I will add them to our food stock and fix a meal fitting to serve the Emperor of China. Who is your cook? I will need help to feed this army of mouths."

A delicious banquet was held. The table groaned and sagged with steamed breads stuffed with dark sugar, noodles, rice, Chinkiang ham, beans and bean sprouts, millet soup, oysters, abalone and gallons of hot tea.

Tom had never consumed such exquisite and rare foods. He ate until his stomach was comfortably full and then beyond that until gorged.

He conversed little, satisfied to merely sit near the wall and listen to the banter and story telling of the men caught up in a happy evening by the companionship of visiting countrymen. He was pleased that he understood much of what was said. It was a very enjoyable time.

The men slept shoulder to shoulder, the normally crowded space barely holding them all. Early the next morning, Guofeng and his group prepared to leave.

The goodbyes were much subdued. Tom understood why. These men might never see each other again. This America was a perilous place for the men from China. Outlaws robbed and killed them, they drowned when ships sank crossing the seven thousand miles of tempestuous ocean and the land itself was hostile and took its toll.

Guofeng gave a last salute to Sigh and Tom and struck out along the return trail. His men fell in behind him like iron filings to a magnet. They vanished one by one into the frosty mist.

The ice cloud began to thin late in the seventh day of the new year. Tom felt his mood brighten as sun dogs began to flash, small incomplete rainbows shining in the diamonds of the frost dust.

The sun came out completely for a handful of minutes just before it dropped behind Black Mountain. It turned dark swiftly, the winter day holding little time between sundown and star-shine.

Tom sat late in front of the dying coals of the fire and listened to the cold cough of the wind on the clapboard roof. It seemed the wind was trying to tell him something. Time and again he got up to broodingly peer outside at the star-blown wilderness night. He saw the moon rise round and frozen and wintry wan.

He sensed his stay with the Chinamen was ending. Yet he felt a bleak loneliness at the thought of leaving.

He was still awake when the false dawn arrived, when a spectrum of the light of the still hidden sun was reflected down into the valley from a high layer of clouds.

Sigh awoke and came to stand in the doorway beside Tom. "You are thinking of other paths to follow, rather than staying here with us," he said.

"Yes. As soon as the weather breaks, I will go."

"What is your route, your destination?"

"I do not know."

"Do you have any money?"

"No. Not one cent."

"You have helped us to mine gold. Some of it belongs to you. How would you like to earn additional money? There is something very important you could do for us."

"What is it?"

"I have asked my uncle in China to buy a woman and send her to America. He is a trustworthy man and will accomplish this for us. She should arrive in San Francisco in March or April. You are the one person who could bring her safely to us here in this place."

"One woman for all of you?"

"We are lonely men, and san doys, bachelors. We have only enough money to buy one woman. We will treat her kindly. Will you do this for us?"

"Certainly. I would be pleased to do it."

"Good. We will talk again of this and make our plans when the days grow longer and the snow melts."

They remained standing quietly in the doorway. On the Snake, the ice cracked and moaned as it strained and thickened with the pressure of the cold. On the mountainside, a scream, like a woman in terror, tore a hole in the cold morning. The cry mounted and peaked and echoed back and forth between the canyon wall before it reluctantly died away.

"What was that terrible sound?" asked Sigh.

"That was a mountain lion. Perhaps it failed to make a kill and now must sleep with an empty belly."

"It is easy to fail," said Sigh. "Tom, do you think we will fail in returning to China with our gold?"

"I don't know. You must keep your guard posted every day and night when the trails are open. I believe Yutang and Guofeng were right and we should have killed the thieves, so they could not return and harm you."

CHAPTER 11

Keging smiled, her lips partly open and her black almond eyes luminous as lanterns, shining with inquisitive innocence. She held out her hands and beckoned to Pak.

The dream was so tangible, Pak put out his arms to pull her to him. Then he jerked awake.

He lay on the hard bunk in the tiny cabin of the clipper ship and stared into the darkness. The ship tossed under him as it drove ahead in a rough sea. The blanket separating Keging's portion of the cabin from his swayed with a soft, rustling sound. As if she were shoving aside the flimsy partition to come to him.

Pak sat up and swung his feet to the wooden deck. He reached and touched the blanket. One long step would take him to her. He craved his cousin's woman. He could not stop the craving.

He took his short sword from where it lay on the bunk. He tied the leather loop of the scabbard around his neck so the sword hung inside his blouse and down between his shoulder blades. No Chinaman could bring weapons, either knives or guns, onto the ship. Pak had asked the Chinese cook to smuggle his sword on board. The man had readily agreed to do it—for a captain in the Hung Society. He also readily accepted the piece of silver Pak offered him.

Pak went out into the darkness on the stormy deck. He walked aft along the starboard side of the ship.

It was the beginning of the second month at sea and three thousand watery miles separated him from Canton. Pak had purchased passage for Lian and himself on the clipper ship, American Wanderer. For the fabulously expensive price of two hundred American dollars, he had obtained a small cabin on the mid-deck of the tall-masted sailing ship. That cramped cave of a temporary living place forced him within an arm's length of Lian almost every hour of the day and night.

Pak paced the empty deck, eyes slitted against the cold rain and sea spray. The ship sailed beneath a black overcast. A stiff wind blew from the starboard quarter and the vessel heeled to port. The oaken beams of the ship creaked. The canvas sails on the three tall masts above his head now and then snapped like muffled pistol shots.

He turned across the fantail of the ship. He thought of the three hundred and fifteen Chinamen packed in the lowest decks under his feet. They had bought passage in the steerage for fifty dollars each. They were men dreaming of golden fortunes to be made in California, and in the meantime, living a squalid and harsh existence in the bowels of the ship. Their only opportunity to breathe the clean sea air was when they were permitted to come onto the top deck in shifts for an hour each day.

Pak stopped by the lee rail to watch out into the turbulent sea. His nose sniffed the wind and his tongue tasted it, tangy and heavy with salt. He had found a liking for the sea.

The ship rolled far to port as it sank into a trough, and a liquid mountain of water rose to loom high over Pak. He half saw and half sensed the menace of the wave and knew afresh the feeling he sometimes had in battle, of how narrow was the gulf separating life and death.

Then the remarkable clipper ship with its tons of lead ballast in the keel pulled itself erect and only the lip of the danger brushed Pak, a thin wavelet coming on board to wet his feet. The Americans were skilled craftsmen to build such a masterful ship.

He turned and walked forward on the tossing deck. He enjoyed the violence of the motion. The winter storm and the ship's struggle through it, was somehow removing some of the tangle that his desire for Lian had twisted into his thoughts.

The seaman on watch made his way among the swaying hammocks in the stuffy fo'c'sle. He held his coal oil lantern up and peered into the face of one of the sleeping sailors.

"Tolman, time to wake for the midnight watch," said the seaman.

Tolman growled something the seaman could not decipher, stirred, then relaxed and began to snore.

"It's your turn at the helm," said the seaman in a louder voice. "The Chief said you'd better relieve the watch on time."

Tolman did not respond. The seaman set his lantern on the deck and reached out to rip the blanket from the man in the hammock.

Tolman instantly sat up and glared about. "Damn you, Standage, I'm going to knock the hell out of you. You don't have any right to do that to a man."

"Before you start swinging at me, you'd best listen. I did just what the Chief said. It's your turn at the helm." He threw the blanket back to Tolman and left.

Tolman swung out of his hammock and dressed in the dark. He went up the ladder to the main deck and headed along the passageway. He detoured to go onto the weather deck to get a fresh breath of air to fully awaken before going to the wheelhouse.

As Tolman passed through the hatch, the ship lurched and rolled steeply. His hand missed the hold on the edge of the hatchway and he was flung out onto the deck.

He saw the figure of a man exactly in his path. Tolman fell upon the unknown person.

Pak saw the man hurtling from the black opening of the passageway. He instantly bent forward to avoid any thrusting knife and to take the man's weight without being knocked over. He struck powerfully upward with a flat right hand, fingers extended and rigid, into his attacker's stomach.

The body of the man settled heavily on Pak. Swiftly he heaved upward. The man went flying away from Pak, striking against the taut cables of the standing rigging extending down from the mast to the deck of the ship.

The man agilely bounced off the ropes on his feet and whirled to face Pak. Without conscious thought, Pak's hands flashed to the back of his neck and found the handle of his sword.

"Stop! Hold up! Damnation, fellow, I didn't mean to fall on you," yelled Tolman. He spread his hands in a mollifying way.

Pak did not know the meaning of the man's words, but he understood the gesture of the empty hands. The ship had rolled suddenly just before the man had slammed into him. It was merely an accident. He released his grip on the sword and walked off along the deck.

"Goddamn heathen Chinaman," Tolman said under his breath as he tenderly felt his aching stomach. He looked at the ropes that had kept him from going overboard. He had been godawful close to going to his everlasting death. "Damn little bastard," Tolman cursed and hurried to the wheelhouse.

He relieved the seaman at the helm, repeated back the heading to be steered and began to curse.

"What's rankling you?" asked the chief, who stood looking forward through the large porthole of the wheelhouse.

"Nothing. Nothing at all," replied Tolman.

"I told Standage to take your blanket if you were hard to get awake," said the chief.

"I know. It's not that," said Tolman as he turned the helm slightly to starboard to maintain the heading against the push of the sea.

The duty officer entered the wheelhouse, spoke to the chief and took a seat at the navigation table. He began to plot on a map under the yellow glow of the gimbaled oil light.

Ziyang, the crewman in charge of the Chinese passengers, came into the wheelhouse. He approached the duty officer and saluted, "Mr. Connel, may I speak with you?"

"Certainly, Ziyang. What is it?"

"One of the passengers has died."

"When?"

"It must have occurred since my last round at dark, Sir."

"That makes three so far this voyage."

"Yes, Sir."

"What did he die of? Is it contagious?"

"I do not know yet, Sir. The body is still below decks, far back in one of the corners. The death was reported to me by one of the passengers."

"Bring the body topside at first light. Have the ship's doctor examine it and report to me."

"Yes, Sir," said Ziyang.

"Chief, I'm going to catch an hour of sleep in the storm cabin. Wake me at four bells or sooner if anything arises that needs my attention."

"Yes, Sir," said the chief.

Connel left through a hatchway in the rear wall of the wheelhouse.

"Ziyang, who is that Chinaman with the woman in the cabin midships?" Tolman asked.

"I only know what little I heard while we were docked in Canton. His name is Pak Ho. Why do you ask?"

"I accidentally fell into him on the weather deck. He hit me in the gut and tried to throw me off the ship. If it hadn't been for the riggin' lines, I'd gone deep six, that's for sure. I'm goin' to crack that little bastard's head as soon as we hit port in San Francisco."

"That will not be an easy task to beat him in a fight," responded Ziyang.

"Why not? I'll pick him up by the pigtail and bash his head in."

Tolman saw Ziyang shake his head in the negative and remembered how quickly the small man had reacted and the pounding force of his hands. There was still a sizeable lump in his stomach from that blow. Also, he had lifted Tolman as if he were air and threw him aside.

Tolman said to Ziyang, "Now if there is something about this man that your old shipmate should know, you'd better tell me."

"He is a captain in the Triad soldiers. He is a highbinder, a professional warrior. I would not want to fight him even if I had a knife and he had nothing except his hands."

"You exaggerate," snorted Tolman. "And what in hell is a highbinder?"

"He coils his queue high on his head and binds it there before he goes into battle."

"Well, highbinder or not, he's going to pay for hitting me for no good reason." I will be careful, thought Tolman. Perhaps the best way to hurt him is through the woman.

Pak walked the deck during the cold, late hours of the night. When daylight arrived over the water, he returned and entered the cabin.

Lian was awake and dressed. She reclined on her cot. As she sewed some garment, her small body adjusted easily to the roll and pitch of the ship. The tantalizing nearness of her presence was like a physical force pressing on Pak. He sat on his bunk and watched her.

She glanced up with that peculiar, composed stillness of hers that Pak had grown so used to, and smiled a welcome to him. The beauty of the smile almost compelled him to smile in return. He looked away with a jerk of his head.

She laid her fingers alongside her cheek with a gentle, thoughtful gesture. She believed she understood his action and shrugged a little and turned back to her sewing with a young woman's shy smile.

Pak lay down upon his bed and shut his eyes. He knew he could never speak of his feelings to Lian. However, he would not care if the voyage lasted to eternity as long as she was there, just across the cabin.

The sky cleared and turned blue and the weather warmed for three days. The Snake River began to grumble and strain beneath its thick covering of ice.

Tom found a vantage point on top of a boulder on the shore and awaited the imminent breakup of the river ice. He sat half-dozing in the soft rays of the sun.

A multitude of crackling, crisp and sharp, commenced. They started near the center of the river and, growing ever louder, spread closer to the banks.

Where the current was most swift, the ice thundered apart in a great, gaping fissure. Water flooded up through the breach and air holes and flowed on top of the ice sheet.

There was a ripping, tearing sound as the ice struggled to pull itself loose from the grip of the shore. The broad plain of the river ice shattered and became hundreds of ice blocks, churning and grinding one upon the other. In a cold confusion of water and ice cakes, the river moved, a tidal wave heading for the ocean.

For a long time Tom remained on top of the rock, watching the river throw off its winter covering. As the day ended, Sigh's discussion with him about going to California and bringing the woman to the valley, came into his mind. The world was a big place to explore. He might as well start in California. In a week the snow would be melted from the low land along the river and on all the south facing slopes. He would leave then.

"It is very beautifully drawn," Sigh told Tom as they bent over the deer hide map. "Where did you get it?"

"My father made it for me," replied Tom.

"Was he an artist?" asked Sigh, marveling at the form and content of the map.

"No. Just a man with a quick and accurate hand."

"It appears to me he has shown direction and distances between places very accurately. I have traveled over some of the land and know those things are properly positioned."

"I have tested it some and found it true," responded Tom. "Tell me the best way to go to California?"

"A person could go west across the mountains to the ocean and take a ship to San Francisco. I do not know that way. I can describe the overland route to California, for I have walked it and on part of it helped build a railroad."

"We are about here," Sigh touched the map with a finger. "Go south beside this big river that flows just outside our door until it swerves southeast and opens up into a valley that is miles wide. From what you have told me, you have already passed over the terrain to that point. From there on, hold a course south to cross the Malheur River. Continue south to find the Owyhee River. Stay on the west bank and keep heading into the noonday sun." Sigh's hand traced a line over the map.

"There is a stagecoach line from Winnemucca to Silver City and Boise City along the Old Paradise Valley Road. Somewhere about here you should find it. Follow it south to Winnemucca, which I judge should be located just off the map here. California is a long distance to the southwest.

"If you want, you can take the train from Winnemucca to Sacramento. A boat carries passengers down the Sacramento River to San Francisco. I suggest you take the train and boat. They are fast and pleasant to ride."

Sigh's fingers moved over the face of the map and back to the location of the cabins on the Snake. He went over the same route, adding details. Tom felt his desire to go exploring grow as the man talked of the high mountains and rivers and large towns with many people.

Sigh finished describing the course of travel. "When will you leave?" he asked.

"Tomorrow morning. It is the last of February. Though there may be more storms, they will be short. Each day should grow warmer."

"I have measured the gold we have dug since you have been here. This is your share." Sigh handed Tom a leather pouch weighing two pounds or more. "When something is divided into thirty three parts, there is not much for each of us. Here is another quantity of gold to pay you to bring the woman from San Francisco. Each man has contributed two ounces. The expense of her passage over the ocean from China and lodging in San Francisco has already been paid. Only the cost of the boat to Sacramento and train to Winnemucca remain. I hope this amount of gold is sufficient."

"More than enough. I am glad to do it for you."

"See the merchant of Chinese foods, Quan Ing on Dupont Street in San Francisco. He will know where the woman is. Most likely she will have arrived by the time you get there. Here is a message that will tell Quan Ing who you are and that you are to be trusted."

Tom put the letter sealed in waxed paper into his saddlebag. "I should be back here by the time the season turns to summer."

"We will be waiting," replied Sigh.

CHAPTER 12

Tom left the camp of the Chinamen at daybreak. He was dressed in his own clothes and a coat Hoy had cut from a blanket and had sewn for him. He was armed with pistol and rifle. His black hair had grown longer and was tied behind his head with a leather thong.

The Chinamen filed down to the gravel bar to work as Tom headed up the Snake River. He looked back at the shanties where his flight had brought him those many weeks past.

The foreign miners were motionless near the river. Sigh and several of the others raised their hands in farewell.

They are a fine bunch of men, thought Tom. He turned away from his friends and spoke to the black horse. It went willingly at a trot on the winding river trail.

The animal was soft after loafing all winter and Tom halted early in the evening. He made camp where the trail veered away from the Snake and went across the foothills of the Wallowa Mountains to Baker City.

Each following day the horse grew harder. By the fourth day, the mustang had hit its stride and developed traveling legs.

That night Tom camped at the hot springs on the Malheur River. There was a gray stone house of two stories little less than half a mile west of him. Tom wondered if it had been there on his trip north and he had not noticed it in his delirium.

He heard voices coming from the house. This was the first habitation of white men he had seen for months. He thought of riding over to visit with the people. However, he was enjoying the time away from other humans and instead searched along the bank of the river until he found where the hot spring water mixed with the river and was cooled to a temperature that was pleasant. There he bathed and soaked in warm comfort for a long time before he rolled into his blanket.

He awoke to a stiff wind blowing out of the northwest. The weather was soon to change. He broke camp quickly and headed straight south over lava hills weathered and covered with tall grass bleached by the winter to a dirty gray.

Twenty miles later his route descended into the valley of a creek flowing east toward the Owyhee River. The wind was somewhat subdued in the creek bottom. He pulled rein and stopped to let the horse rest and graze for a while.

Tom took his rifle from its scabbard and found a seat that allowed him to watch both ways along the creek. Snow had drifted into the gully and a mound of white remained at the shadowy base. Tom scooped up a handful, compressed it into a lump and began to eat.

He relaxed and listened to the wind clawing its noisy way over the hills above him. The wind gradually shifted, working its way around to come directly out of the north. It gusted down into the ravine to rattle the parched reeds of grass and strum a thin whine through the lava rock.

The wind strengthened, steadied and began to turn cold. Its whine became an endless moaning dirge.

Then abruptly it changed. A sound unlike anything Tom had ever heard was combined with the dismal tune. He cocked his head to listen.

The additional notes were similar to the first wind noises, and yet different, more controlled with certain resonances accented as if to bring forth emphasis in a deliberate and artful manner. The new notes were full of lament and spoke of sadness.

Tom slowly rotated his head from side to side. He could separate out the sound superimposed on the natural wind noises. And he knew the direction of its source.

He climbed erect and stealthily crept up the drainage. The sound grew louder. He dropped down and began to crawl.

He stopped and parted the dry grass to peer ahead. A skinny old man with white hair sat at the feet of a bony nag of a horse. He held an odd-shaped instrument with wire strings beneath his chin with his left hand. While his right drew a flat bow of some material over the taut strands of metal.

His eyes were shut and his seamed, hatchet-thin face was concentrating on his task.

The wind intensified, shrieking a wild song, and the old man's music rose to match and mock it.

Tom was astounded. Never before had he heard a fiddle. He had seen pictures of them in books and his father had described the music such a wooden box made. However, now with the vibrations of the strings reverberating in his head, he knew his imagination had failed significantly in fully understanding the beauty of the music a fiddle could make. He wanted the man never to quit playing.

But he did stop. The bow ceased its stroking of the strings and the fiddle was lowered. The old fiddler man climbed up to lean on the horse.

Tom saw the man's face. Weather and time had blown and crumpled him into ruin. The thin body and spindly legs and arms reminded Tom of a frail grasshopper walking on the autumn frost, knowing that winter and death were close.

The man retrieved a battered carrying case from the ground and made to stow his fiddle in it. Tom arose from the grass.

"Hello," Tom called.

The ancient fiddler man spun around. Keen blue eyes caught Tom and measured him. The man had been startled, but he had not shown fear. Tom liked that.

A genial smile came to the face of the fiddle player. "Hello, yourself, my young friend."

"That thing you hold, is it called a fiddle?" asked Tom.

"Fiddle be damned, this is a violin." The man examined Tom's earnest visage, then shrugged. "Yes. Let's call it a fiddle. In this place and time, that is a fitting name."

"It could be called a violin in some places?"

"When I played before the princes and crowned heads of Europe, they definitely referred to it as a violin."

"You make very pleasing sounds from it," said Tom.

"Sounds?" the man cried. "I make music. I am the best violin, er, fiddle player in the world."

"I meant music. I have never heard music before."

"You are a man grown and never heard music. You lie."

"I never lie," replied Tom, taken aback by the man's harsh words.

"I'm sorry I said that. It is possible you have been deprived of a great inheritance of man."

"Would you play some more for me?" asked Tom.

"My price is high. When I was on tour giving renditions of classical compositions, I was paid much gold."

"I don't understand your rendition of classical compositions. But I have only a little gold. I will give you some of it."

The man smiled in unbelieving amazement. Was the youth telling the truth? Yes, for it was in his face. "Gold out here has little value. Perhaps this is something else we can barter. What direction do you travel?"

"South."

"And what is the name of the place you go?"

"California."

The man's countenance brightened. "If I might join with you in your journey, I would play a tune for you all the way. Let me give you some samples."

The fiddle went in under his chin and he settled his head. The bow stroked across the metal strings and the man's fingers walked about in a skillful manner on their ends.

Tom saw the man's eyes tracing the broken lava rock at the top of the ravine, and his music rose and fell in sharp abrupt tones, presenting the outline as if in a picture. He played and drew the blades of grass dancing in the wind, the trickling brook chasing through the rocks at his feet.

The fiddle strings moaned with the wind, gloomy and cold. The man noted the somber expression come onto Tom's face and he intensified the sorrowful tone, playing with the youth's emotions, pulling them to the surface.

When he saw Tom's eyes become misty with some remembrance, the old fiddler relented. He launched into "Buffalo Gal," giving its normal fast pace an additional lilting quality that soon had Tom patting his knee.

Tom glanced into the fiddler's eyes. He understood the old man had been toying with him. He smiled his comprehension and nodded his acceptance of the trick.

"You can come with me," said Tom. "What is your name?"

"John Kelly. And what is yours?"

"Tom Gallatin." He put out his hand and shook the man's.

"My horse is old and I have no food," declared John.

"How did you get into those straits?"

"Men often stop working at what they do best to try new adventures. Almost always the change is a mistake. I was at Morman Basin digging for gold when I should have been playing my fiddle. Working in the cold water of the creek made my old bones ill. For weeks I could not rise from my bed. When at last I could stand and the weather turned somewhat warm, I decided I would go to California with its balmy winters. I struck out on the road. My horse got into deep water on the Malheur River and I lost my food supply. I have no money to buy more."

"Tough luck," said Tom. "I have enough for two until we can find a place that has provisions for sale."

"Good," replied John. "What town do you go to in California?"

"San Francisco."

"I go to Los Angeles. It is located in a wonderful land for an old man to spend the rest of his days. It is south of San Francisco so we can travel together most of the way."

"Then shall we be off and riding?"

"A little food would be nice to start our trip," John said.

"Why sure," said Tom. He untied his grub bag from behind the saddle and spread enough for two.

Tom and John rode long that day through rolling hills with cottonwood and willow in the draws. They made silent camp in the edge of night.

John was trembling with fatigue as he unbound his two blankets, both thin as an old woman's skin.

"I have an extra covering you can use," said Tom, handing John his blanket. "I have my wolf-skin sleeping robe. It will be enough for me."

"Thank you. The storm is getting worse. It will be a cold night."

"I will build a fire out a few feet in front of that big, square rock," Tom said. "Put your bed there between the rock and the fire and the heat reflecting from the rock will help keep you warm. There is plenty of cottonwood. It burns up fast, but I will drag in a big pile of it before darkness comes."

"I think I will lay down now," John said.

"Sure, go ahead and rest."

Often during the night, Tom awoke to shove the long poles of wood farther into the fire as the ends were consumed. Each time he would look upward expecting the storm, but all he saw were the stars glittering like ice shards flung across the ebony sky.

In the small hours of the morning, the wind became a violent blast and shadows rippled through the night as clouds chased across the heavens. The clouds thickened and a dense overcast came in beneath the moon.

All the next day, the north wind shoved Tom and John across rough hills. Heavy-bellied clouds weighted down with snow scudded above them. The end of the day came early and the darkness was so heavy it pressed snow from the clouds.

They were up and riding with the first coming of dawn. As the day lengthened, the storm gathered madness and fury and the snow thickened and streamed down. Drifts formed and grew in the lee of every rock and bush. They climbed up a mile-high ridge where the sky was an ocean of swift white wind.

Tom was worried about the old fiddler man. He glanced backward, squinting into the storm that roared over them. John sagged in the saddle. Some of his long, white hair had escaped from under his hat and was dancing and flicking into the wind. The web of wrinkles was imprinted so deeply in his sallow face they looked like scars. Wind tears were ice upon his cheeks. Shelter must be found soon or the man would die.

"Your horse needs rest," Tom told John. "Ride my black and I'll walk for a way."

John stared at his young companion for a long time. He nodded his understanding at the kindness being given him. He dismounted and pulled himself astride Tom's horse.

Tom could see nothing beyond a couple of hundred feet. He thought the wind still blew from the north. He put it to their backs and descended the slope to the bottom.

Another hill obstructed their path. Tom guided the way up to its round top. In that exposed elevation the wind clouted them and diamond ice, hurled against his bare skin, stung like flame. He rested but a moment on the hill, then mounted John's horse. They went onward down from the hill with snow plastered to their faces and wind pounding their backs.

Where the land flattened, Tom halted and his frozen eyes wrestled with the drifting phantom forms of snow. Unbelieving, he saw a house. In front stood a stagecoach, its hulking one-ton bulk rocking to the slam of the wind upon its tall side.

He checked the chimney. Smoke rose up, barely clearing the chimney top before it was shredded to bits by the wind.

Tom walked close to John. "We have found a house. They have a fire."

John raised his head and looked. He exhaled a fragile breath into the frigid air. In a voice thin as a ghost's he said, "It's a stage station."

They sat their horses in the lonely gloom of the blizzard, not yet fully believing they had found shelter.

Saddle leather creaked as John took hold of the pommel and tried to dismount. "Tom, I'm going to need some help. I don't think I can walk," he said, his teeth chattering with the cold.

Tom lifted him down in his arms and carried him to the entrance of the stage station. He kicked the door. In a few seconds, someone moved aside the protective block on a gun port cut through the wooden portal and stared out at him. The door swung open and Tom entered with his burden.

The room was large. Low benches were stretched along one wall. Four small tables, handmade of wood, were placed on the right side of the room. A large dining table was in the center of the room just off an alcove where a cooking stove could be seen. Through an open door at the rear of the room, a man was visible sleeping on a bed. All the windows were shuttered with thick wooden planks.

Groups of people were scattered here and there at the tables and on the benches. Tom ignored all of them. He carried John straight to the big, pot-bellied iron stove next to the side wall. Gently he set the old man on the earthen floor.

Within the stove fire crackled. Flickering flames cast yellow light out through the draft hole to dance on the floor.

John leaned forward and breathed a lung full of the warmth radiating from the fire. He shivered once more, gave Tom a kindly look from those faded old eyes and smiled. "I think I'll live a little longer now and be able to keep my promise to play you some tunes on my fiddle."

"That's good," responded Tom. "You rest. I'll take care of the horses."

Tom faced the room. "Who's the manager here? I've got two horses that need to be gotten into cover and given a ration of grain."

"You got any money?" questioned a square built man at a table containing some papers and a cash box. He gazed doubtfully at Tom's dilapidated clothing.

"Got gold," replied Tom.

"All right, then. Round back is a long shed with plenty of stable space. Find a place there for your animals. You can get grain from the sack in the corner near the mangers."

"How about food for my friend and me?"

"Pot of hot beans and beef there on the stove. Part of a roast chicken on the table. Plenty of tea and coffee there. Some boiled eggs left, too. My woman is baking more bread. She'll set you a plate when it's done. You can spread your blankets right there where the old man is."

Tom nodded and went outside the door. He led the mustangs into the long, low building and gave each animal a full gallon of grain and an armload of hay. As they greedily crunched the grain between their broad teeth, he stripped saddle and bridle from them. Carrying John's bedroll and gear and his own, he headed back to the station.

Tom stopped at the stagecoach and circled it, examining the vehicle stoutly built of oak and iron. The leather curtains were drawn and he could not see inside. Promising himself a more complete investigation of the coach later when the storm let up, he walked to the station building.

The building was of two types of materials. The older section, and the largest, was of wood. An addition on the right was of stone. Gunports showed in strategic places on all sides Tom could see. A solid little fortress. He went inside.

"Find everything you need?" asked the manager.

"Yes. What's the name of this place?"

"Rattlesnake Station on the Hills Beachy Stage Line."

"Big crowd of people. All passengers?"

"Stage had to lay up because of the storm. Be moving on,

probably by tomorrow. The driver is catching up on his sleep now. My woman says she is ready to feed you."

John and Tom ate a hearty meal and then spread their beds on the floor. The old man instantly went to sleep.

Tom looked around at the other people in the room. Three soldiers in cavalry uniforms sat talking at one of the small tables. Three men in miner's clothing were playing poker with a pack of frayed cards. Two cowboys and two young women laughed and conversed with each other in high, good spirits. In one of the corners, an Indian lay flat on his back, sleeping and snoring in a low rumble.

The wife of the manager was visible in the kitchen alcove in the old section of the station. The manager was silently making entries in his ledger.

"This stage heading south to Winnemucca?" Tom asked the manager.

"Yep. About one hundred and eighty miles. You're a strong looking fellow. You looking for a job? If so, there's plenty of work there, for the town is booming since the railroad arrived last year. The pay is three dollars a day for carpenters in Winnemucca and four dollars at the new gold mines in the Tuscarora Mountains."

"Nope. Not looking for work. Just passing through. I'd like to buy two tickets."

"You're in luck. Only two seats left inside the coach. Looks like your old friend couldn't ride another mile in this cold and snow. That'll be sixteen dollars apiece for a total of thirty-two."

Tom brought out his gold and the man carefully weighed out the correct amount on a small scale. "Here are your tickets. Keep them and show them to the driver at each stop if he asks to see them."

"How much to board my horse for a month or two?"

"Didn't you come on two horses?"

"One is old and not worth anything. I'm just going to turn him loose."

"The Company does allow us to help people who take the stage and need a horse waiting for them when they return. Charge is two bits a day. They get grain and hay."

"It is a deal. My name is Tom Gallatin and I'll pick the horse up myself."

He returned to John and stuck one of the tickets in the band of his hat. He put the second one in his shirt pocket.

John awoke in the evening. He threw off his blanket and grinned at Tom. "I've had food, a fine sleep and I'm warm. You provided this for me. How would you like to hear some music?"

Tom smiled back at the old fiddler man. Only the heartwood of him remained, all else whittled and wasted away. But he endured. "Don't play anything sad," Tom said.

"How about a rendition of a world classic?"

"You must explain what that means one day, but for now play one."

John's blue eyes laughed and his mouth curled into a happy smile as his practiced hands drew the bow so beautifully across the strings of the violin.

CHAPTER 13

The music of the fiddle came softly and pleasingly. Tom was relaxed, leaning back against the wall and letting his mind bask and revel in the lovely tones.

John finished the piece and Tom opened his eyes. "Why does music always cause a person to remember things of the past?" Tom asked.

"I hadn't thought of that before, but I believe you are correct and most tunes do recall old memories. Are you ready for another?"

"I can listen longer than you can play."

John began. Several of the other people in the room had ceased talking and craned their necks to listen.

"Louder," called one of the cavalry soldiers. "Play louder so all of us can hear."

The fiddler increased the volume and everyone became very quiet. The bow moved in his practiced hand for several minutes without stopping. When he finally ceased, the women clapped approval. The men joined in.

Tom knew the applause was well earned. He was stirred in a way never before experienced. He was glad he had found the old man and they traveled together. What other pleasant mysteries waited for his discovery?

The manager's wife lit the coal oil lamp on the dining table and smiled at John. "Now you can see to play your fiddle some more for us."

"Thank you for the light, but I need none. My fingers and the bow know the notes of the pieces of music so well they can play them equally well in the dark." He chuckled. "And if that wasn't so, I would simply compose my own."

"Don't all people play music they make themselves?" questioned Tom.

"Very few have the artistic touch to create their own music. Some of what I have played for you was written by others."

John spoke to the assemblage of men and women. "Something to dance by, would that meet with your favor?"

"Great idea," said one of the cowboys. He arose and put out his hand to gently pull one of the young women to her feet.

At that moment, the outside door swung open and two men in heavy sheepskin coats, with hats pulled low against the storm came into the station. The wind flickered the lamp and snow swirled inside with them in a little blizzard before they could shut the door.

They were rawboned men with full beards. As they unbuttoned their coats to receive the warmth of the fire, tied down six-guns were exposed. They held their hands to the heat and stared in a measuring manner at every man in the room.

John played a lively tune with a beat. The manager and his wife, and the two cowboys and their women danced in the lampshine. The cavalry men and the men in the miner's clothing patted their feet in rhythm.

Tom watched the movement of the men and women to the music and the smiles upon their lips. A pleasant emotion caught him. One day he would learn to step in that peculiar fashion.

The tune ended. The dancers looked at John to see if he was going to play some more. But the rough strangers, who said not a word and stared about, had somehow put a damper on the festive mood that had prevailed in the room. John seated himself on his blanket and placed his violin beside his hat on the floor.

Tom closed his eyes. He was tired after fighting the storm for hours. He dozed off, replaying the last tune in his head.

The manager reseated himself at his table and his wife went into the kitchen. The cowboys and their women found seats and soon a flow of conversation started.

One of the new arrivals approached the manager. "Two tickets to Winnemucca," he said.

"Sure," said the manager. "But you'll have to ride outside the stagecoach."

"What do you mean?"

"All the inside seats have been sold."

"It's too damn cold for a man to ride outside. It's below zero out there."

"The driver does."

"Maybe so. But he gets paid and dresses for it. Me, all the clothes I've got with me are what I got on. I want to ride inside."

"The stage runs three times a week. If you want to wait, there'll be another one in two days."

"I'm not going to wait. How about the Indian? Is he going on the stage?"

"The Paiute, that's old Broken Horn. He's going to Fort Mc-Dermitt."

"Then we'll take his ticket for one of us," said the man.

"The Indian rides for free and he rides on top," replied the station manager.

"Then just sell me two tickets for inside."

"There are no seats, like I told you."

"You don't understand. You sell us the tickets and we'll trade with somebody," said the man.

"No one will trade with you," said the manager.

The man put his fists on the top of the table and leaned over the seated manager. "Hear me for the last time. Sell me two tickets."

"Sure," muttered the manager and handed over the tickets.

The man returned to his comrade and said a few words to him. Both turned to cast a calculating stare around the room. Their eyes roamed over the three cavalrymen, the miners, and the cowboys.

The first man spoke in a quiet voice. "Stokes, I'm sure the old man and boy wouldn't mind swapping tickets and riding outside."

Stokes chuckled a wicked laugh. "You're right, Terpin. And it wouldn't make any difference if they did."

"Watch the others and back my play," said Terpin. He strode up to John and bent to remove the stagecoach ticket from the band of the hat lying on the floor.

John had been watching the pretty faces of the young women until the man had drawn near. Now in surprise, he grabbed Terpin's hand to prevent him from taking the ticket.

Terpin shook off John's clutch and slapped him in the face.

"Just take it easy, old man. I'm going to trade you seats on the stagecoach." He reached for the ticket. As he did so, his fingers struck the strings of the fiddle and a sharp discordant note rang out.

Tom came instantly awake. He saw Terpin's fingers near the fiddle. Tom reached and clamped the man's hand in a viselike hold.

"Don't break the fiddle," Tom said.

The man yanked back, trying to pull free. Tom arose with the man's motion, coming immediately to his feet.

The man tried again, jerking powerfully to wrench away. Tom squeezed the hand harder and twisted. The man winced.

Tom knew from the first tangle that he was the stronger. He caught the man's other hand.

"Don't make any fast moves," Tom warned. He plucked the six-gun from the man's holster and tossed it on the floor.

Tom spoke over his shoulder. "John, what's going on? Are you all right?"

"He was trying to steal my stage ticket," answered John. "When I tried to stop him, he bloodied my nose."

Terpin saw the eyes of the youth, only inches from his own, suddenly take fire and burn with fury. Then a hard fist smacked him in the face.

"Now he has a nosebleed, too," said Tom. He looked quickly at the man's partner.

That man was sidling sideways trying to get a better view of him.

Instantly Tom pivoted Terpin left to put him more completely between himself and the second man.

Tom cried out in a voice like steel striking steel. "If you move again, or reach for your gun, I'll kill you."

"I don't bluff easy," hissed the man.

"But you'll die easy." Tom was outraged at the meanness of the two men. He felt the wolf rising in his heart as he had that day when the thieves had tried to take the Chinamen's gold. He flung the first man aside and stood poised.

It seemed the distance separating him from the threatening man diminished by half as he focused on him. That every living thing in the room became immobile and time stood still.

"Stokes, kill him," shouted Terpin through the blood gushing from his nostrils and cascading over his mouth and chin.

"Yes. Kill me if you can," said Tom. The feeling of anger ran through his mind like arctic winter. The urge to begin the fight himself grew rapidly.

John looked up at the young man who moved with such deceptive swiftness and strength. He sensed the building desire of Tom to do battle. John's own heart began a wild tattoo of flutters. He believed Tom could kill the man and he did not want him to do that.

"Let him go, Tom. Don't shoot him because of me," John said.

At the old fiddler man's calm voice, Tom grappled with his anger. It was difficult to hold in.

"It's not worth it," said the old man. "Let him go."

John was correct, Tom knew. A cold wind seemed to blow through his brain and the violence in him was whisked away.

"Get away from me. Get out of here," Tom ordered.

Stokes hesitated, evaluating Tom. The immense confidence of the youth was sapping Stokes's courage. Some animal instinct told him he would be lucky to get out the door alive. He left at a run.

Terpin made as if to retrieve his six-gun.

"Leave it," ordered Tom. "Go while you can."

The man hurriedly moved through the door after his partner.

The manager went to the door, shoved it closed and dropped a heavy bar into place to secure it. "They are two goddamned bastards," he said.

Tom took a seat beside John. Now that the danger was past, his heart hammered on his ribs. The killing had been a near thing.

"Thanks, John, for stopping me from shooting them," Tom said. "But we got his nose bloodied damn fine."

The driver was awakened and brought from the only bedroom in the station. The women retired there for the night. The men slept on the floor of the main room.

The sky in the morning was a brilliant blue, swept clean by the passing arctic storm. The temperature was far below freezing. The snow crunched beneath the iron-shod hooves of the prancing coach horses as they were led from the stables. In the rays of the bright sun, frost on their winter coats of hair sparkled like a thousand tiny jewels.

The three teams of horses were backed into position on opposite sides of the tongue of the stagecoach and the trace chains hooked to the single trees. Baggage was brought from the station and crammed into the boot in the rear of the coach or tied on top.

"Bundle up in your heaviest coats and get aboard," shouted the driver. He scampered up the front wheel and into the driver's box. He threaded the reins between his fingers and looked down at the passengers as they loaded into the coach. The Paiute scrambled up over the luggage in the boot and settled himself among the boxes and bags on top.

There were four bench seats in pairs situated crosswise the coach. Tom took one next to a window. John sat beside him and one of the cowboys occupied the third seat. The two women and the other cowboy sat facing them. The remaining passengers found space in the facing seats in the other end of the coach.

The long bullwhip cracked and the rested horses, invigorated by the cold, left the station at a run. Snow swirled up and trailed the coach in a white, billowing tail.

The driver soon pulled the horses down to a trot and went directly south on a well-used road through slightly rolling grassland.

The coach lurched as it dipped into a small gully crossing the road. The young woman opposite Tom was jostled and her knee rested against his for a moment. She smiled at him and drew away.

Tom could not remember ever being so near a woman. This one was very pretty and not much older than he. From then on Tom did not know which he enjoyed the most, the lovely woman directly in his line of sight and whose leg touched his from time to time, or the delightful stagecoach ride. He did know that the thought of her kept him warm in the cold drafts that came in past the window curtains of the coach.

Shortly before midday, the stage halted at Summit Spring. The passengers and driver had lunch and fresh horses replaced the tired ones. The horses were changed again at Ten Mile Creek. The snow-covered Steen Mountains were passed upon the far borders of the western sky at dusk.

Once darkness came, it seemed to Tom that the woman's leg touched his more frequently. Finally, after a hard jolt, the warm pressure of her leg remained pressed to his. He made no effort to draw away. He was exhilarated and he knew his heart was racing. Why did the mere touch of her do this to him?

Fort McDermitt, sitting astride the Oregon and Nevada border, was reached in the snowlight of a high, cold moon. The stage stopped in front of the yellow, lighted doorway of the station. The passengers climbed stiffly out after many hours of travel.

All the luggage and parcels were removed from the coach. The soldiers gathered their belongings and walked away into the dark and snow. The women and the cowboys left shortly thereafter, off along the street.

Tom felt a loss at the going of the woman. He watched after her, thinking she would look back. Not once did she turn her head. She disappeared into the night with her friends.

Tom pondered over the girl for a few seconds and then shook his head. His father had told him very little about females.

Tom glanced at the dim outlines of the buildings lining the street. He wished it were not dark so he could see the town.

"Food's ready," a woman called from the lighted doorway of the stage station.

"How are you holding up?" Tom asked John.

"Fine. I can stand anything knowing California is getting closer."

"Are you hungry?"

"Yes. If you have enough money, let's see what they have prepared for us."

They dined with the other passengers on roast beef and potatoes, boiled eggs and the flesh of crab. "See what I told you," said John and pointed at the crab. "The ocean and California are getting nearer."

The woman cook heard John's words and spoke. "With the railroad at Winnemucca and ice every place, it is easy to get seafood."

"And crab is my favorite kind," responded John, taking another serving.

The replacement driver came to the door of the station. "I'm loading the luggage now. The stage leaves in ten minutes."

There was a last foray on the food and the passengers filed outside. Tom was amazed, for in the light shining from the door, he saw a larger and nearly new coach.

The body of the coach was a bright red and the undercarriage a rich yellow. There were splendid, thick cushions on the seats. Still, only twelve passengers could be seated. The extra space was taken up by army pouches, mail and other special parcels that required speedy transport.

The stagecoach left on the blackness of the night. It plunged south along the Quinn River into a bleak and lonely land.

The terrain was an intermontane basin, an area as large as France from which no streams flowed, an area where once gigantic north-south-trending blocks of the earth's crust had been thrust upward, and then eroded and carved by wind and water into long mountain ranges. The rivers that were born on the mountains all flowed into miles-broad alkali flats of the lowlands and there dwindled away to nothing in the sands.

Four hours later, Flat Creek Station was reached. Tom got out to stretch his legs and stood in the snow while a change of horses was being made. In the starlight he could tell the land was wide and open to the west. The giant bulk of a mountain, the Santa Rosas, one of the passengers had said earlier, blocked out the stars on the east.

Ahead there were deeper shades of black where the valleys of streams came down from the mountain. Those would be dangerous to cross and a wreck could happen easily in the dark. Still, the skilled driver and the night-seeing eyes of the horses were keeping them all from harm.

His father had told him about stagecoach travel. He had not mentioned that a portion of the journeying would be in the night.

The coach moved swiftly behind trotting horses in the cold morning hours. It rode easily, rocking on the leather through-brace shock absorbers. Tom dozed.

The sun came up over the high Santa Rosas and evaporated the darkness. Tom opened the leather side curtains and stuck his head out the window to view the country.

The Quinn River lay three or four miles to the west. The tall

Santa Rosas to the east were carrying the morning sun on their rocky spines. Ahead past the trotting horses, the valley of the Quinn River stretched onward for a dozen miles before it veered west.

Soon the road swerved southeast and climbed up into a pass cutting through the rugged Santa Rosas. Just as the grade broke to the east, the stage reached Willow Point.

Horses were swapped and the coach rocketed down the eastern grade into the glistening, snow-covered Paradise Valley. The last battleground of the Paiute nation, where two years before the U.S. Army had finally caught and conquered the hostile warriors.

The stage drove directly south, paralleling the Little Humbolt River and its braided channel. The road ran on the wavecut terraces and beaches, marking the shores of an ancient sea that once, twelve thousand years before, filled the valley hundreds of feet deep.

Small herds of cattle and bands of sheep grazed the tall, wild rye grass in the river bottom. Some ten miles farther east, the Hot Springs Mountains were visible. Immediately behind them, and towering over their lesser neighbors by half a mile, were the Osgood Mountains.

The stage drew to a halt at the main Humbolt River. Both banks were lined with thick ice extending ten feet or so out into the water. A four-man work crew, two men on each shore of the river, were chopping at the ice with axes. Beneath the slashing blades, the ice shattered and sailed away in sprays of silver shards.

One of the workmen hurried up to the driver. "We've finished cutting the path for the horses and stage. Whip them up so you get a run at that steep far bank."

"Damnation," cursed the driver. "I know how to drive these horses. Get the hell out of the way."

With a wild yell from the driver and the nine-foot whip popping near the ears of the horses, the coach plunged down the bank and into the ice and water. The driver lowered the metal end of the snapping bullwhip to touch a lagging steed. The animal surged forward to tighten his traces.

The solid vehicle rattled over the stony bottom of the river

ford and bounced up the bank behind a scramble of driving
hooves. A minute later, with a squeal of brakes and taut reins, the
stagecoach came to a halt at the station in the center of Winnemucca—the site the Shoshone people had once called, "Place
by the Water."

The town consisted of sixteen boxlike wooden buildings on the
south bank of the Humbolt River. The structures lined a snow-
covered dirt street that extended a short distance up a low grade
to the south. Three miles beyond the termination of the main
street, the ten thousand feet high Sonoma Mountains rose precip-
itously out of the grass and sagebrush desert.

Tom and John stood on the only stretch of sidewalk in the
town, a fifty-foot section of wood planks running in front of the
stage station and the hotel next door. Hammers rang in the cold
desert air at half a score of buildings under construction. A large
structure of three stories was nearing completion near the railroad tracks.

"Not much of a town right now," said John. "But it soon will be.
The coming of a railroad and the discovery of gold always makes
for boom times. I'll bet that big building by the tracks is a new
hotel. They always build them close to the depot."

Tom remained silent for he had no comparison to make.

John continued to speak. "However, San Francisco and Sacramento are real cities. You will be seeing them soon."

"Let's find out when the next train leaves heading west," said
Tom.

They shouldered their gear and tramped along the streets to
the train depot.

The agent of the railroad at the depot answered their question.
"The train leaves daily for Sacramento at three P.M. You have
about a half hour to wait."

"John, we haven't really rested for more than a day and a half,"
said Tom. "Do you want to sleep for a night or catch the next
train out?"

"What do you want?" countered John, looking out over the
sere cold emptiness of the valley.

Tom grinned. "I'm anxious to get on with the journey. I've a
woman to meet in San Francisco, and I'm sure there is much to
see and many things to do there."

"Good. Let's take the first train. We'll catch what rest we can on the move." John felt an urgency to not delay, for there was a tremble of weakness running throughout his body. His limit of endurance had been exceeded and he was traveling on raw nerve alone. He did not want to gamble on becoming more ill and dying in this grim land. He would make California or perish on the way.

CHAPTER 14

The locomotive gave a shrill whistle, a belch of steam, and its driver wheels began to grind for grip on the iron rails. Towing three passenger coaches and two mail cars, the engine crept from the Winnemucca Station.

Tom settled back upon the upholstered seat beside John and watched out the window. The speed built and the sound of the wheels hitting the joints of the rail sections grew to a rapid, unending series of dull clicks. The snowscape glided past faster than the swiftest horse could run. Altogether a very pleasant sensation of movement.

The conductor in his black uniform came through the coach, collecting tickets. He stopped for a moment at the metal stove in the center of the car and stoked it full of hot burning pinewood.

Tom smelled the newness of the railroad car and the pungent odor of the pine resin bursting into flame. He was pleased at the comfort and speed of the train.

"John, I believe I'm going to like this way of traveling," Tom said.

"It certainly has advantages over horseback and stagecoach travel," agreed John. "I've heard the Central Pacific has all new locomotives and coaches on their portion of the transcontinental run."

Tom watched the passengers swaying to the motion of the car. Nearly all the seats were full. He recognized only the three miners of the stage ride.

John brushed his hands tiredly across his eyes. "I think I'll try to get some rest now," he said.

Tom looked closely at the pale, old man. He was obviously very ill and yet not once had he complained of the many hours of arduous riding on the cold, jarring stagecoach.

"There's more than enough seats for everybody," said Tom.

"I'll find another one. You take all this space and stretch out the best you can." Tom stood up and walked forward to the seat behind the miners.

John took his bedroll from the floor at his feet and extracted a blanket to use as a pillow. He lay down.

The voices of the miners talking among themselves reached Tom. One said, "In fact each year since the foreign miners' tax was passed into law in '66, my collections have increased."

"Mine have, too," a second man said. "I bet there are at least three thousand Chinamen in Oregon. Nearly all are mining. They're panning away on just about every stream that's showing color."

"How much tax have you been collecting?" asked the third man.

The first man laughed. "Do you mean what did I turn in to the state? Well, now let me recall. In July I tried something new. I hunted Chinamen in the night when they came into their camps after working the creeks. That was a poor month. Only collected eighty licenses. In August I got rough. Had me a China fight. Knocked some down and pulled my iron on the rest. They put out then. Took twenty-nine hundred dollars. September, collected about twenty-four hundred dollars. October, three thousand dollars. Had a great time that month, cut off several Chinamen tails."

The second man spoke. "In November I took in forty-one hundred dollars," he bragged.

Tom stopped listening. The men were tax collectors. Sigh had told him of the fee Chinese had to pay to mine gold in Oregon. The charge was four dollars each quarter of the year. Tough men were hired by the state to search the creeks and collect the tax.

Often the tax was collected more than once. Dishonest men, declaring themselves agents of the state, tramped the canyons and made forcible demands on the foreigners. In retaliation, the Chinese did what they could to hide the true numbers of men in the work groups.

The train sped southwest beside the Humbolt River. The mountainous upthrust of the Humbolt Mountain Range, with Star Peak stabbing like a spike into the sky, passed on the left.

The more rounded dome of the Trinity Mountains slid by on the right.

The Humbolt River was crossed at Carson City. West of the city, the foothills diminished and faded away and the train raced out onto the broad expanse of the Carson Sink. This was the graveyard of the Humbolt River, a three-thousand-square-mile area consisting of sand dunes circling wide alkali flats that in turn surrounded, in the lowest depths of the sink, mile upon mile of marshland.

The thundering and hissing locomotive sped near several shallow lakes and sloughs. A great white cloud of snow geese rose up, to be immediately joined by masses of gray crane, green-head merganser duck and the many-colored widgeon, and scores of other species of waterfowl.

Tom was flabbergasted as the heavens became black with soaring, milling flocks of birds, each crowding the other for sky room to fly. Never had he imagined there could ever be so large a multitude of waterfowl.

The train veered due west from Carson Sink and approached the Pah Rah Mountains. Just before the climb started, the locomotive pulled onto a siding and stopped. A thin white haze rose around it as excess steam was vented.

As the passengers waited for the oncoming traffic, the sun weakened and the evening dusk came rushing from the east and overran the motionless train. A few minutes later the eastbound train sped down the mountain grade and swished by an arm's length away, a dark blur with flashing patches of yellow light from the windows of the passenger coaches.

Water and wood was replenished at Reno. The twisting, tortuous climb of the straining locomotive up the mighty Cascade Mountains was made in the night.

Morning arrived and lit a dazzling new world of snow and evergreen forest. The train wound through the large pine, fir and spruce and reached the crest of the mountain range. Tom's view was quickly drawn beyond the mountain to a mammoth valley that seemed to stretch forever to the west. He began to wonder if he might not actually be seeing the ocean at that farthest reach of his eyes.

The train tipped toward the balmy Pacific and began to pick up speed.

Sacramento lay spread across the flat flood plain of the river with the same name. It bustled with activity as drays, wagons, hacks, carriages and coupes moved endlessly along the streets. The hurrying townsfolk, though seemingly bent upon important business, still often called out greetings to each other.

"A magnificent city," said John and waved his hand to indicate the entire assemblage of buildings and the thousands of acres of irrigated cropland ringing the town. "It is the capital of California and, with the coming of the railroad, is the center of transportation and trade in the state."

"I have never seen anything like it," said Tom. "Thousands of people must live here."

"Yes, indeed, tens of thousands. Let's go down to the dock and catch the riverboat to San Francisco. That city on the coast hills is even more beautiful."

They moved along the wooden walkway in front of a wide variety of business establishments and arrived at the river shore. A brilliant white riverboat tugged gently at the hawsers that held it to the wharf. People were filling up a gangway to board at the bow. At the stern, carriages and saddle mounts were being loaded by way of a stout wooden ramp lowered from the side of the boat.

"We have now returned to civilization and my fiddle has once again become a violin," said John and smiled at Tom. "Now let me return some of the kindness you have shown me and I'll pay for our passage to San Francisco. Keep my gear while I talk with the captain of yonder vessel."

The captain stood midship near the side rail and called out orders to members of his crew. Now and then he greeted a dignitary or a friend. He ignored the attempts of the rickety old man on the pier trying to capture his attention.

John opened his battered violin case. He lifted up the violin and tucked it in under his chin in that certain way Tom was so familiar with. Even at his distance of a hundred feet on the noisy pier, Tom heard the lovely music commence. A waltz, John had once called a similar tune.

Heads began to turn. Traffic near John halted. He played for twenty seconds and halted in the middle of an ascending bar.

The captain was looking at John with interest. They conversed briefly.

John turned and motioned for Tom to come. They took places in the line of passengers and without a ticket boarded the riverboat.

The last arriving passenger came up the gangway and onto the deck. The captain took the helm and the vessel cast off its lines and drifted away from the dock. A whistle tooted and the steam-driven paddle wheels started to churn the water.

The captain steered the broad-beamed craft far out on the river, searching for the deepest water. Finding it on the outside sweeps of the meanders where the water current flowed fastest and scoured the bottom.

"Now to keep my bargain with the captain," said John. He walked out to the center of the deck and raised his violin.

He played for a quarter of an hour, a medley of one captivating tune after another. The passengers at the far ends of the boat congregated around him and remained silent and enthralled for the total time. The applause was deafening when John finished. Tom greatly admired the iron will of the old man to put on such a performance even though sick.

John stood motionless with his eyes closed for a moment, recovering his strength from the effort. People had noted his weakened condition and his worn and frayed clothing. Now they began to toss silver coins, quarters, half-dollars and big heavy dollars to rain upon the deck at the old man's feet. At first he appeared not to hear the ring of the coins striking. Then he looked about and gave all the friendly throng his wide and kindly smile.

The loudest accolade had come from a group of four young men on the lower deck. Now they opened a keg of beer in the rear of their carriage and lifting full mugs above their heads, began to sing in good harmony.

Finishing the song in high, good spirits, they invited those people near them to find something from which to drink and join in emptying the keg.

"Shall we go down and sample the brew?" John asked.

"I'd like that," responded Tom. He would miss the courage of the old fiddler man when he left and went on his way to the city called Los Angeles.

San Francisco was a city built on sand hills adjacent to a wide and shallow bay. A broad avenue, The Embarcadero, paralleled the shore. Many streets ran directly west from the thoroughfare and up the steep grade of the hill. Several rackety wooden piers extended east of The Embarcadero, hundreds of feet out into the water.

Each wharf was jammed with drays loading and unloading and seamen and craftsmen speaking a Babel's tongue of languages. Steam pile drivers were hammering long timbers into the bottom of the bay for new piers. Chuffing paddies were hauling sand from alongside the piers to deepen the water so the ships could come closer in to the land.

Scores of warehouses, large and cavernous, crowded the shoreline. Beyond that were the offices and business buildings stepping off along the streets. The brightly painted homes of the town residents were higher on the hills.

John and Tom entered the Coastal Steamship Company office on the wharf at the end of Market Street. John bought a ticket for his trip south to Los Angeles.

"Go right on board," said the attendant. "The last call before sailing has already been made."

John grasped Tom's hand. "I owe you my life. For that I most heartily thank you. It is very unlikely we will ever meet again. I wish you a long and happy life."

"Perhaps you will come with your music to San Francisco before I leave and I will see you then."

"I do not believe that will happen. But I would like to leave some advice with you about San Francisco. It is a very large city, probably one hundred and fifty thousand people. It has a great vitality, a dangerous energy. It is a wicked city with many rough and crooked men—and women. There is little law enforcement to control the scoundrels, drifters and rogues that have been drawn here. Only a few policemen are on the streets. Fearless Charlies they are called. Be very careful and trust no one."

"I can take care of myself," responded Tom.

John looked at his young friend with the bedroll on a shoulder, a rifle hanging lightly in a hand and a six-gun on his hip. Where he came from, he was a formidable opponent. Here in this place where crimps, muggers and every kind of sharper had a hundred tricks to throw a man off guard, Tom was an innocent.

"Especially stay off The Embarcadero and the Barbary Coast, that's a stretch of the Pacific, Kearney and Broadway Streets. You are just what they . . ."

"Mister, you are going to miss your ship," yelled the steamship company employee.

John squeezed Tom's hand one last time and hurried away. He boarded the steamer and went to the stern.

Tom waved at him as the ship left the dock. John lifted his hand in final salute. Oh, if only he were young again, what a pair he and Tom would make!

The schooner *Tenrun Bay* wallowed on the end of its anchor chain as the tide reached that instant of time when it was in equilibrium, moving neither in nor out. Then slowly, ever so slowly, the high tide began to run out of San Francisco Bay. The schooner swung to the current, coming up with a little jar on the end of its chain and headed toward the beach.

Captain Boorstin slapped the railing a resounding smack of anger. He had brought his ship heavily laden with cargo from Maine around the Horn and north up the coast to San Francisco. The profit was great. But never again would it be, for the railroad was now connected coast to coast. He could not compete with that.

Other ships were making great profit by taking goods to China and hauling back a live cargo of Chinamen anxious to get to the golden mountains. It required little time for him to decide that was his next voyage.

However, within one day of arrival in San Francisco, all his crew but four had deserted, jumping ship and rushing off to the gold fields or taking shore jobs that paid three times the wages a crewman drew.

The tide ran stronger. It swirled and gurgled around the canting masts and spars sticking up above the water from dead ships, abandoned by gold-crazy men, and now sunken and forgotten on the bottom of the bay.

A coastal steamer, riding the outgoing tide, chugged past close on the port side. An old man with long white hair blowing in the wind stood by the railing and looked backward at the docks.

"Dotson, come here," ordered the captain.

Dotson, the first mate, came along the deck. "Yes, Captain."

"We've been waiting two days for more crewmen and Sam McNair hasn't sent one man or a word of what he's doing. We can't keep those poor bastards he has already delivered tied below decks forever."

"Aye, that we can't," said the mate. "Some of them are bad hurt and need fresh air."

"Go ashore and tell Sam not to wait for someone to come to the boarding house or the saloon. Tell him to send his best crew of people out on the street and find me three strong men. Damn it, I want those men so I can sail on the morning tide."

"Captain, that's dangerous to try and knock men over the head right on the street. A Fearless Charlie might see them."

"I know it. Tell Sam I'll raise my price to a hundred and fifty dollars a head if he delivers tonight. And also tell him I'll bring him a bolt of the best silk in Canton for his woman."

"Right, Captain."

The mate walked aft to where a skiff rode to a short line. Nimbly he went down the Jacob's ladder and cast off the skiff. Bucking the tide, he rowed for the shore.

The captain shouted after him, "Tell Sam not to break their skulls. I'm going to be short-handed even with three more men, and I don't want a bunch of cripples trying to handle sails."

CHAPTER 15

"Take plenty of cartridges for your guns," Keggler told his gang of six men. "You'll soon have a lot of use for them. We're going to kill us a bunch of heathen Chinaboys and take their gold."

Keggler paced the floor as his men finished packing their bedrolls and saddlebags. He held his head angled to the right and slightly raised to ease the torment of the pain from the damaged vertebrae in his neck. Not once since that day on the Snake River when the big Chinaman had injured him had the agony left.

The winter months had seemed endless to Keggler as he waited for his revenge. But now the weather was sunny and for the first of March quite warm. The snow was melted and the ground thawed. He was not going to delay any longer for the mud to dry.

The outlaw chief spoke sharply to Bassel, the Boise gunman he had taken into the gang to replace Cardone. "Damn it, hustle yourself. The sun will be at the top of the sky before you get ready to ride."

Keggler glanced at Crowe, the replacement for Vaughn. He stood in the yard ready to ride. He was a quiet man who took orders well and was a fierce fighter when the fracas started.

"Mount up or get left behind," barked Keggler and climbed into the saddle.

The seven outlaws left at a gallop, splashing the sloppy mud. Keggler's blood ran hot. He would be killing his enemies in only one day. No damn Chinaman was going to lay hands on him and not pay for it with his life. And as for the white kid, Keggler would personally shoot him.

The sky remained clear as the gang skirted the Wallowa Mountains. In late evening the Snake River was reached and the men turned to ride with the current. When they came to the big oxbow of the river, they halted and climbed stiffly down. A camp without fire was made on the riverbank.

"We'll be there and looking down our sights at the moon-eyed Celestials by mid morning," said Keggler. "We break camp first daylight, so be ready to travel."

"The Chinamen have posted a lookout," said Keggler, peering through the grass on the crest of a rise of ground upriver from Sigh's mine.

" 'Pears he has a rifle. Probably one of ours they took last winter," responded Ottoson, who lay beside the bandit chief.

"The guard's not too smart about his job," said Keggler. "He's in the open where he can be seen easy. Also, there's brush close to his back. Can you slip up on him and kill him without his sounding a warning to the rest of them?"

"Sure. Give me a quarter hour to get above and come down behind him," replied Ottoson. "I'll put a knife in him real quiet like."

Ottoson crawled back from the top of the hill and made his way down the slope to the ravine at the base. Bending low, he skulked up the depression eroded in the mountainside.

Keggler glanced up the Snake River at the hiding place of the rest of the gang and all the horses. Nothing was visible to ruin the surprise. He lay where he could see the guard and waited for Ottoson's assault on the man.

Guofeng alternately ran and walked through the brush and boulders on the bank of the Snake. His heart beat pleasantly, for he was a happy man.

A pouch of gold, tied around his neck, tapped gently on his chest as he moved. The gold was the reason for his swift pace toward Sigh's camp.

Guofeng had discovered a new placer gold deposit, one that had never been worked and was rich enough to make half a hundred men wealthy. The nuggets in the bag had been simply picked up from the pool of water at the mouth of a spring.

The fluvial deposit containing the precious metal was long and narrow, extending for hundreds of feet along the Snake River at the base of Triangle Mountain. Several swift streams tumbled down the steep flanks of the mountain, scouring their bottoms to bedrock and cutting the gravel bar into sections.

That segmentation had created the problem. Guofeng did not have enough men to work all the sections at one time. Other prospectors might come and lay claim to some of the gold-bearing gravel not being mined. To forestall that happening, Guofeng wanted Sigh to send men to join his crew and work the entire length. That would protect Guofeng's discovery rights, at least against other Chinamen.

Guofeng heard the metal clatter of shovels hitting rock and he slowed to a walk. Sigh's camp was just ahead.

Before Guofeng had gone a body length, a rifle crashed. He flinched as if he had been struck. A horrible premonition seized him. He sprang forward through the brush.

A fusillade of rifle shots roared, many weapons firing. The sharp explosions hammered and echoed on the walls of the valley.

Guofeng halted at the edge of the thicket and peered out. His friends were running in all directions across the gravel bar. Bullets hit, knocking some men off their feet to lie crumpled and motionless.

Part of the bullets missed their intended targets, striking the stones and ricocheting away, snarling like deadly little animals.

Some men, wounded and knocked down by the heavy slugs, struggled to their feet and, in stunned bewilderment, staggered erratically through the hail of rifle fire. Then, before they could escape harm's way, they were pierced again, to fall in death.

One man sprinted straight for the river to evade the deadly ambush by swimming the swift current. A chunk of zipping lead caught him in the back of the head and he fell in the shallow water. With his feet still on the shore, he made feeble, swimming motions with his hands. Then even that ceased.

Guofeng saw Sigh dash to crouch behind the boulder in the center of the bar. Sigh grabbed the golden cube from the top of the rock and bent low, darted up the course of the Snake. The gods seemed to be favoring him, for bullets struck on all sides of him and still he ran untouched.

On the ridge above the camp, a man with a rifle rose up from some screening bushes and ran across the side of the mountain, parallel to Sigh's course. However, on the rough slope the rifleman could not keep up and Sigh began to draw away from him.

The man stopped, knelt and raised his gun. The weapon cracked. Sigh stumbled sideways as the bullet punched through him. He made three steps and fell.

He raised back up and, bent far over with pain, trotted slowly up the river. The gunman on the ridge shot again. Sigh collapsed on his face and did not stir.

At last the firing stopped. Bodies lay strewn in grotesque slumped forms. A man moaned. Another sat up and dazedly looked about.

Guofeng lay down and raked dead grass and leaves over himself. He was shivering. Never had he felt so sick. But he would not leave; he must see all the horrible things that happened here so he could tell other men.

Keggler stood up from his hiding place and motioned to his men. "Let's go down and finish the job."

The outlaws fell in behind their chief. As Keggler moved through the wood yard of the Chinamen, he picked up the chopping ax and took it with him.

"Fan out," ordered Keggler. "Check all the bodies. Take the live ones over there by that big rock."

Keggler went at once up the river to where Sigh lay. He had seen the Chinaman grab something and attempt to escape with it. He had almost made it. But Keggler had made a lucky shot at a long distance.

The outlaw chief kicked the toe of his boot in under Sigh's body and flipped it over to lie face up. The golden cube lay shining on the sand.

Keggler laughed deep down in his chest. "Well, you little sonofabitch heathen, I've got your nugget."

He quickly looked around at his men. None were close or watching him. He ripped a broad strip of cloth off the tail of Sigh's blouse and knotted the yellow metal cube in the center. With the loose ends, Keggler firmly tied the treasure around his waist, inside his shirt and coat.

Again Keggler checked his men. All were occupied with examining the Chinese miners.

Keggler took up the ax and raised it above his head. He whispered at the dead man. "You damn Chinaboys liked to break my neck. Well, now I'm going to chop yours off."

He swung savagely down on the exposed, slender neck of Sigh. Then swiftly again to complete the decapitation.

He dropped the ax, caught hold of the corpse's clothing at chest and ankles and flung the small body into the river. He threw the head many times farther, to land with a splash.

"Feed the little fishes," said Keggler and laughed wildly. He was still laughing when he walked with the bloody ax in his hand to join his men.

"Four men still alive," said Ottoson and pointed at the men sitting propped against the boulder. He saw his chief's face, saw the smiling happiness there. This was a damn bad play and Keggler laughed. The man had remained unconscious for two days after the fight with the Chinaman. His behavior had changed since then; he had become short-tempered, violent. Ottoson wondered if he was working with a crazy man.

"Did anyone see a white man or a big Chinaman?" asked Keggler.

"Not me," responded Ottoson. "And no one escaped."

All the remaining gang members also answered in the negative.

"Well, we'll make these four tell us where their gold is," said Keggler. He squatted in front of them with the ax in his hands.

"Where is the gold hidden?" Keggler asked the nearest Chinese.

Wong, the man who had shown the nuggets in the store in Baker City, did not understand the words, but he knew what the question was. He had felt fear as the bullets had zipped past during the firing and even greater fear when one struck him. Now that fright left him. He would be dead in a minute. It would be good to die before the other injured men. It would have been much better to have been killed first of all his friends and countrymen, for he was responsible for all this tragedy.

"Where is the gold?" the outlaw chief questioned fiercely and lifted the ax up to rest on his leg.

Wong looked at the bandit and showed his teeth in a grimace of a smile.

Keggler savagely hit the Chinaman on the face with his fist.

Wong rolled sideways to the ground. When the bandit chief sprang up and raised the ax, Wong reared back his chin to fully expose his neck.

"I am sorry, my brothers, for your deaths," Wong said to the three wounded men watching him with scared eyes. He hoped many others lying lifeless on the bar could somehow also hear his stricken apology.

"Make a clean cut," Wong said in Chinese to Keggler.

"Goddamn heathen think their gold is worth more than their lives," exploded Keggler.

The members of his gang moved uneasily as they stared at the ax.

"Don't chop them with the ax, shoot them," said Ottoson. "That's a more natural way to kill."

Bassel spoke angrily. "Maybe they know they are all going to die regardless what they tell us."

"Both of you shut up," hissed Keggler. "One of them may understand what you say."

"None of these is the one that did the talking the last time we were here," said Ottoson. "I bet these can't talk American. Even if they could, they won't tell us anything."

"You're right." Keggler's voice had a shrill edge. He kicked the remaining three men onto their backs and stood over them gripping the ax in both hands.

All the Chinese miners, except Wong, tried to scrabble away on hands and knees. Keggler followed after them, the blood lust hot and red in front of his eyes. The sharp silver blade of the ax arced down, falling again and again upon one man after another.

"That's three more Celestials without heads," muttered Keggler.

He moved to Wong, who had not stirred during the murder of his friends. "You are the last one," said Keggler and swung mightily with the ax. The bit sliced all the way through Wong's neck, crashing into the rocks of the bar to send sparks flying.

Keggler pivoted about to stare at his men. "Any one of you want to make something out of this?" He tossed the ax away and let his hand hang close to his six-gun. "Come on! Speak your mind. I can outshoot any of you. Any two of you."

He looked at Bassel and Ottoson. "You are plenty quiet. You'd better stay that way. Now, before a white man comes by and sees all these dead men, throw every one of the bodies in the river." Keggler laughed in a high-pitched voice. "Without bodies, no crime can be proved."

The band of men hesitated to touch the corpses. Keggler jerked his pistol and pointed it at them.

"Do what I say or I'll send you to join them. Bassel, take hold of that man and drag him to the river."

When Bassel did not move, Ottoson spoke. "Best we do what he says. We've killed our share here today."

"When you are finished with dumping the bodies, start searching for the gold. Break up everything usable or burn it. Leave nothing for another bunch of Chinaboys to use."

"I've found the gold," cried LeRue, running out of the cook shack and holding a leather bag up for all to see. "It was buried in the corner of the kitchen."

"Let me see it," said Keggler.

He extracted two pouches from the bag and opened each. "There's dust in one and nuggets in the other," he said.

"Where is the big nugget we saw that first day?" questioned Ottoson. "That's the thing I want to feel in my hands."

"It's not here," replied the chief. "I think these fellows were some of the smart Chinese who took their gold to town for safekeeping after they accumulated a goodly sum."

"How much gold do you have there?" asked Bassel, motioning to the quantity Keggler held.

Keggler hefted it in his hands. "About three hundred ounces."

"Damn little pay for the sorry thing we've done," said Bassel. "You said there'd be a lot of gold. Hell, I could make my share of that gold in one night stealing horses."

"Look again for the big lump of gold," said Keggler. "We'll burn the buildings when we are finished."

Later the men congregated with glum faces. Ottoson spoke. "Absolutely no more gold anywhere. Not one pinch."

"We're not going to find it," said Keggler. "Best we get out of here. Get the horses and let's ride."

"Not to Boise or back to Baker," said Ottoson.

"That's right," Bassel added. "We must go someplace far away. We can watch the newspapers and listen to word of what is said about this thing we've done to the Chinamen."

"Right," agreed Keggler. "Then when all is quiet here, we will come back and take this gold mine and hire a bunch of Chinaboys to wash out the ore. I say we go to San Francisco. I hear that's a big town and has got some good doctors. Maybe one can fix my neck to stop it hurting. Burn the shanties and let's ride south."

Guofeng cried as he lay under the brush and watched the bandits ransack and burn the cabins, bedding, clothing and demolish the sluice boxes.

He saw the swinging ax and the mayhem the bandit chief wrought on his friends, the grisly decapitations. His countrymen had been thrown in the river, never to be returned to China and buried in the fertile black soil of the Pearl River Valley.

He had listened to the conversation of the killings, but only the name of the city, San Francisco, did he comprehend.

When the bandits were far up the river and out of sight, Guofeng climbed to his feet and wandered grieving among the burning buildings, looking at the blood-stained rocks where the bodies had fallen. Sigh and the others had been slaughtered as though they were animals. The God-cursed bandits must be punished.

His own camp was miles away to the north. There would be no help at that place even if he could return there swiftly. Only the officials of the white men could bring the murderers to justice.

He considered his own group of men. They would be leaderless without him. What of the rich gold strike at the base of Triangle Mountain?

His men and the gold would have to wait. He would follow the killers until they came to a place where men would believe him when he told of the frightful murder that had been done here on the river. An awful thought arose in his mind. Would anyone believe him?

Guofeng retrieved his small pack. It was not sufficient for a long journey. He began to sort through the ravaged possessions of Sigh's camp.

A half-burned blanket was raked from a smoldering fire and

the hot embers beaten from the cloth. He salvaged some spilled rice, raisins and other foodstuffs from the ground. Matches, another partially charred blanket and a coat that had somehow missed destruction were added to his growing mound of supplies.

Guofeng bundled all his provisions and tied them securely. He fashioned shoulder straps and hoisted the load to his back.

He fell upon the trail of the horsemen. They were heading south. Perhaps they might go to Baker City. Guofeng knew a few white men there. They might recognize the truth when it was told.

Where the road divided and the right-hand way went to Baker City, the bandits continued straight ahead.

Guofeng followed with implacable determination. Perhaps they were heading for San Francisco, the city that had been mentioned in their talk.

He began to trot, his wiry body striding easily, stepping precisely upon the horse tracks of his enemies.

The second day it stormed on Guofeng. Raking winds drove heavy snow and the temperature plunged to below zero. Guofeng would have frozen that night had he not come upon a rancher's flock of sheep bedded in a creek bottom. He crept among them with his knife. He killed two and skinned them and lashed the thick fleeces into a sleeping robe.

He rolled himself in the thick wool covering and slept warmly. Only his bad dreams of the tragic murder disturbed his slumber of exhaustion.

In the morning he kicked the frozen green hides until he broke free of their clutch. He carried the fleeces with him, and as he walked he scraped the fat and flesh from the raw side until the skins were soft and pliable.

By noon, Guofeng found the tracks of his quarry in the snow. He broke into a steady, ground-devouring trot after them. His hate kept him warm and built a burning energy within. Never would he let the men escape him.

CHAPTER 16

Tom left the docks that extended seaward from The Embarcadero and wandered, interested and watchful, through the throng of laborers, businessmen, drifters and the ever present seamen and ship's officers. All around him the wooden planking of the street rumbled under the hooves of a hundred horses and the iron-rimmed wheels of buggies, drays and massive cargo wagons.

He passed a five-story building on Market Street and marveled at its size. Shortly thereafter, he came to Harpenning Block and the striking Grand Hotel with its four hundred rooms.

In front of the hotel, a middle-aged man in a town suit smiled and said hello to Tom. The fellow looked as if he would be familiar with the city. Before he could move off in the crowd, Tom spoke to him.

"Please. Can you tell me where I can find the store of a man named Quan Ing?"

"I do not know the man. But practically all Chinamen live on eight or ten blocks straddling Dupont Street." He turned to point up the hill. "Chinatown is on that high ground near Portsmouth Square. Go there and ask for more directions."

"Thank you. Dupont Street is what I am looking for," said Tom.

He resumed his course up Market Street and onto Montgomery. Two blocks farther and he reached Dupont Street.

A large sign that read "Chinese Foods, Quan Ing, Proprietor" hung over the sidewalk a short square ahead. The building was narrow and in need of paint. It was wedged in between two structures of like age and character. A bell tinkled as Tom entered.

A young Chinese man sat on a chair at a low counter. Behind him were long series of shelves reaching to the ceiling and chock full of a multitude of varieties of dry goods and foodstuffs and extending rearward into the dark recesses of the store.

On Tom's right a second Chinaman, quite large for his race, sat at a table close to the wall. He scanned Tom and his rifle and pistol and hurriedly reached to pull a small cord hanging from the ceiling.

Tom heard a second bell chime somewhere in a distant part of the building. In only a handful of seconds, two men glided into view in one of the aisles between the shelves and came speedily toward Tom. They were dressed in dark blue clothing very similar to that which Yutang and Sigh and the others had worn. The only difference was the black, round-topped hats on their heads.

Each of the two men had a hand inside his blouse and their faces were alert and hard. The large man by the wall began to close in on Tom. A half-drawn knife showed the steel of its blade.

Tom was surprised at the threatening movements. And he had little time to decide how to respond since the men would be upon him in an instant.

He dropped his bedroll on the floor and stepped forward to lay his rifle on the counter. He lifted his pistol from its holster and placed it beside the long gun. He backed away three paces, pulled Sigh's message from a pocket and held it up for all to see.

Tom spoke in Chinese. "I am looking for the merchant, Quan Ing. I have a letter for him."

The men slowed and stopped. They evaluated Tom silently. Their hands came into view without weapons.

The man on the left spoke in Chinese. "I am Mingren Yang, Quan Ing's assistant." He bent in a slight bow to Tom. "Forgive our caution. You are a stranger to us and sometimes strangers bring undesirable—" He hesitated and then added, "Undesirable events."

Tom bowed—it seemed a very proper thing to do—in acceptance of the apology. "I am Tom Gallatin. Sigh Ho, a friend of mine, has asked me to deliver a message. Would Quan Ing be kind enough to meet with me?"

"I shall ask him. It may take a moment." Mingren bowed again and went off, his slippered feet noiseless on the wooden floor.

Tom relaxed and watched the men. These were fighters. It was evident in the way they moved and in the complete lack of fear with which they had advanced to challenge a man heavily armed with firearms.

Why would a mere merchant have a need for such men? Quan Ing was more than the proprietor of a food store.

One of the guards positioned himself between Tom and the guns on the counter. The other man stood on Tom's right and a couple of yards distant. The clerk had vanished. No one spoke or moved.

In the silence Tom thought he heard the click of abacus beads for a second and then it ceased as if a door had been opened and closed.

Mingren and another person approached from some unseen entrance in the rear of the store. The second man was small, a full head shorter than Mingren. He was old, perhaps ancient. Maroon silk clothed him loosely. Long, wispy chin whiskers dropped to the center of his chest.

The man's eyes probed quickly and intelligently across the space separating Tom from him. Tom bowed to the man as Sigh had told him was the custom when youth met venerable age.

"I am Tom Gallatin."

"And I am Quan Ing." His English was perfect. "Mingren has told me you have a message from one of my countrymen, Sigh Ho."

Tom passed the sealed paper to Ing. Tom shifted to English, since that seemed Ing's preferred language at the moment. "I am sorry it is somewhat dirty and bent, but it has had a long trip."

Quan Ing fitted a pair of spectacles to his nose and tore open the message. He finished reading and looked past the paper to Tom.

"Sigh tells me of the dangerous things that have occurred in your province of Oregon and your part in all of it. I would like to hear more of this. Come with me. It is time for the evening meal and we can talk while we dine. Also, I will tell you of the woman he has purchased."

Ing said to Mingren, "Take Tom Gallatin's possessions to the room next to yours. Then come join us. Station the other men back at their posts."

"Yes. As you direct, Honorable Ing," said Mingren.

"Come with me," Ing said to Tom.

He led the way along an aisle and out a door in the rear wall. The room entered was larger than the one just left.

Four men were at desks calculating numbers from sheets of paper on abacus boards and entering sums in ledgers. Beyond them the room looked like a warehouse. Seven men were packaging various items in bags and wooden boxes, obviously for shipping. Two men sat at a table near a barred door and played dominoes. They immediately sprang to their feet when they saw Ing and Tom.

Ing made a slight gesture and the men reseated themselves. Tom and Ing passed by and went through another door.

The room was splendid with long silk drapes hanging on the walls. Thick mohair carpets covered the floor. The finest wooden furniture, delicate and ornately carved, was placed in a most pleasing arrangement.

The men did not stop there, but continued into yet another room. A long table set with silver, fragile glassware occupied the center of the space. Twenty people, perhaps twenty-five, could be seated at the table at one time.

"You may wash and refresh yourself in there," said Ing and indicated a curtained doorway. "Then return here and allow me to show my hospitality."

Ing, Mingren and Tom were the only people at the table. Two young women served them. Tom lost count of the number of different dishes of food placed before him. He savored the distinct and delicious flavor of each new dish and concentrated on the conversation with Ing.

Ing questioned Tom in detail about the Oregon land, the discovery of gold there and how his countrymen were faring in that faraway country.

"I am saddened by the taxing of Chinese miners. That is unfair. But I understand the reasons behind it, for nearly all my people are merely sojourners in America. Most will one day return to China. However, some, like myself, will never leave. We have become part of all that happens here."

One of the guards who had been playing dominoes in the outer room entered and conversed in a low voice with Ing. The merchant pondered for a moment and then turned to Tom.

"The steamship *Japan* came into port this morning with nearly thirteen hundred Chinese aboard. That has made for a long day for all of us. We are having difficulty finding lodging and food for them. Our dormitories were almost full before this very large shipload of men arrived.

"I must leave you and attend to some of these matters. We will talk early in the morning about Sigh's woman. Mingren will show you to your quarters."

Ing spoke rapidly to Mingren in a dialect Tom did not comprehend and left through a side door.

Mingren guided Tom to a spacious sleeping room. "This shall be for your use as long as you stay in San Francisco. A warm bath has been prepared for you in the adjoining room. If you desire, you may also have your clothing washed while you bathe."

Tom glanced down at his worn and soiled garb. Compared to Mingren and Ing in their fresh, neat garments, he was a vagabond.

Tom laughed and said, "I would very much like to have clean clothes. Tomorrow I will buy a new outfit. I imagine the patches on these clothes are not very suitable for a big city like San Francisco."

Mingren grinned back. "I will give the instructions. Do you plan to go into the city this evening?"

"Yes. There is much I want to see."

"Perhaps you are aware that many sections of the city are not safe after dark. In fact some places are not safe at any time for new arrivals."

"I have heard that. But I'm not worried."

"Then I shall see you at breakfast."

"Is it possible somebody could wake me in the morning? By the looks of the softness of that bed, I might sleep until noon."

Mingren smiled. "Would you like for a pretty girl to awaken you?"

Tom reflected upon the girl in the stagecoach. He had found much pleasure in looking at her pretty face. He thought he could still feel the spot where she had pressed her leg against his. "That would be fine," Tom told Mingren.

Tom leisurely bathed and shaved his sparse young beard. By the time he finished, his clothes had been washed and ironed dry. They were still warm from the hot metal of the iron when he donned them. He wondered how many servants worked behind the walls and how many rooms there were in Ing's home and business. What type of business was Ing really involved in?

Tom knew of only one route to an exit and that was back through the store. He walked in that direction. The guards stopped him at the warehouse section and let him out the side door. Tom heard the iron bolt being shoved into its locking socket behind him. He wondered what Ing was afraid of.

Darkness had fallen on the narrow streets. Stygian gloom filled the cramped alleyways. A cold sea breeze crept among the buildings.

A few people hurried past Tom. The sound of a flute and cymbals playing a weird, alien music came from inside a building on the opposite side of the thoroughfare.

Two blocks later, he saw an old woman wrapped in a thick shawl on a balcony over the street. She was wailing a Cantonese lament of homesickness and rocking to and fro. Tom stood for a moment and watched her and listened to the sounds of the city and its smell.

Tom left Chinatown. He went three squares along Church Street and came out on Jackson Street.

There was fog in this lower elevation near the ocean. The wash of the gas streetlights showed as dull pools in the mist.

He passed a brightly lighted house with a sign naming it Blind Annie's Cellar. Men strolled along the street and entered the establishment.

Now and then a night woman walked by Tom as he continued along the street. Often they looked at him, trying to catch his eye. His attention was not on them and they went on their way.

The fog formed droplets on Tom's eyebrows and his cheeks became wet. He brushed the moisture away. He had never experienced anything like this before. He felt washed in the mist. He began to think that maybe the drippy, misty night streets should be left to the people who knew their way about. He should return to Ing's and do his exploring in the light of the sun.

He came to a streetlight haloed with the wet sea vapor and stopped to get his bearings. A tapping sound came from the window of the house beside him. He turned to look.

A small Chinese woman sat in the window. She was seated on a cushion on the wide sill and tapping on the glass pane with her long fingernails. A lamp was placed on a nearby table in the room so the light would illuminate her.

She smiled as Tom looked at her and turned her head from side to side in the light so he could see how pretty she was.

Tom grinned back. She was a most friendly girl.

She bent and lifted the sash of the window. "Would you like to come inside?" she asked in English.

Before Tom could answer, someone touched his arm. A female voice asked, "Wouldn't you rather make love with me?"

Tom turned and in astonishment stared down at a beautiful young woman. She was dressed all in black, only her blond hair and white face showed, like an ivory cameo against the night.

Her fingers slid down his arm, cool and soft, and took his hand. "Come with me," she said.

Tom went a couple of steps under the pull of her hands; then he halted.

"It is all right," she said. "Come along."

"Why me?" asked Tom.

"Because you are handsome." She put an arm about him. "I will give you a pleasant night." There was a hint of urgency in her voice.

Tom did not move, puzzling at the offer.

She moved closer and hugged him around the waist.

"Watch out behind you. Men come," the woman in the window cried out at Tom.

Tom whirled around at the warning. Three men, moving swiftly shoulder to shoulder, were a few feet distant. Each carried a club in his hand.

Tom's hand flashed down for his six-gun. The holster was empty. Damnation!

The men were almost upon him. He could not let them surround him. He crouched low and charged the middle man.

As he caught the attacker over his shoulder, Tom felt a club hit him a walloping blow on the back. He ignored the sudden pain and drove forward, lifting the man off his feet.

Tom saw the wall of the building swiftly approaching. He butted the man, shoving him ahead to absorb the shock of the imminent collision.

They struck. Tom heard the sodden crunch of the man's head breaking on the brick. The man dropped his club on the cobblestone.

Tom snatched up the length of hard wood and spun to face his assailants.

The men separated and warily, holding their billy clubs poised to strike, eased closer. One man nodded a signal at the other. Both would attack Tom at the same time.

A man dressed in dark clothing materialized out of the fog. He delayed a second, his sight darting over the scene, interpreting the situation. Then he sprang at the back of one of Tom's opponents.

His hand shot out and a long knife sank deeply into the man. He stabbed out powerfully twice more, each time driving the blade to the hilt in the man's back.

The club dropped from the nerveless hands of the man, already dead on his feet. He fell toward Tom, his face thudding on the stone street.

The man with the knife turned and without a backward glance trotted away. The fog swallowed him up.

Tom leaped at the last attacker. The man swung his club. The reach was short.

Then Tom was close. When the man tried to hit him with a backhand strike, Tom broke his knuckles with a blow of the club. Instantly Tom smacked the man on the side of the head with the wooden weapon, and then across the back of the neck as he went down.

Where was the woman? Tom rotated, peering into the foggy shadows. She stood against the wall of the building. She raised Tom's pistol to point at him.

Tom hurled himself aside. As he did so, he flung the club at the woman.

The gun roared, missing its target.

Tom heard the club hit the woman with a thump. The pistol clattered on the street.

The woman cried out and backed away into the darkness. Tom scrambled around on his knees, feeling for his six-gun. He found the pistol and stood erect.

The Chinese woman was yelling at him. "Run! Run! Before you

are caught!" She jerked the window down with a crash and blew out the lamp.

Tom heard shouts and the stamp of feet hurrying in his direction.

He ran.

CHAPTER 17

Tom awoke at the knock on the door. He rolled to his back and sat up in bed. "Come in," he called.

A young and very pretty Chinese girl came into the room. She smiled at him and in pleasant, lilting Chinese said, "Food will be served in one hour. Mingren has asked that I tell you Honorable Ing requests that you come and dine with them."

Tom grinned. Mingren had kept his promise that a lovely woman would be the person to rouse him this morning.

"Thank you," said Tom. "Tell Mingren I will be there promptly." He swung his feet to the floor.

The girl looked quizzically at Tom. "Is there anything else you desire?"

"That is all. Please go and tell them."

She left, looking back as if expecting him to call to her.

Tom felt the bruise on his back. It was swollen and tender to the touch. A blow such as this could have crushed his skull.

He washed, dressed and went to his second-floor window. He was above the fog that lay nearer the ocean. A clear blue sky soared overhead, and the early morning sun threw slanting rays across the town, already awake with a bevy of people and vehicles moving on the street.

Tom watched for a while. Then judging an hour had elapsed, he walked along the hallway and down the stairs to the dining room. Ing and Mingren were already seated and conversing in their native tongue.

"Please have breakfast with us," said Ing and motioned at a chair on his left. "Did you rest well?"

"It was a very comfortable bed. The best I have ever slept on," replied Tom.

"It has the down of duck and geese and should be most soft. I am pleased you enjoyed it."

A woman servant set hot food before Tom. He began to eat with the two men.

"You went out into the city last evening," Ing said in a matter-of-fact statement. "How did you like our city?"

"A friend told me San Francisco had places that a person should go to only in the daylight. I found one of those streets."

Tom looked at Mingren. "Thank you for your help last night. I don't know why those three men jumped me. But they would have likely bashed my head if you hadn't taken that one off me."

Both Mingren and Ing stopped eating. Their faces became studied and noncommittal. They glanced at each other and then back to Tom.

"I do not know of what you speak," said Mingren with a frown. "I did not leave the house after dark."

Tom smiled. Mingren did not want to be thanked. "I recognized you. You did very well with your knife."

Ing spoke. "Mingren is correct, Tom. You must be mistaken in what you saw. No Chinese would harm a white man regardless of the danger to a friend."

Tom flushed hot at his error of judgment. The feeling of resentment and dislike of the white men for the Chinese was extremely high. He remembered the gold thieves on the Snake River. A Chinaman killing a white man could bring much violence and even murder upon the Chinese community. However, he knew with certainty Mingren had aided him in the fight. How else would Ing have known it had been white men in the attack?

Yet Ing was too intelligent to have made such an accidental slip of words. He was, in an indirect manner, telling Tom the precarious situation that existed for Chinese in this land of America. Further, Tom wondered if Ing had not instructed Mingren to follow and keep him safe.

"It was foggy and dark," said Tom. "I did not see the fourth man clearly. Still, one day I would like to meet him so I could properly say thanks."

"That probably will never happen," replied Ing. He paused. "I have received word of the woman Sigh Ho has acquired. Her name is Lian Ah. A man, Pak Ho, a cousin of Sigh, is accompanying her. The information I have is that they were to sail on the clipper ship, *American Wanderer,* approximately three months ago. The ship may come today, next week, or never, for it must come a long distance over a stormy and perilous ocean.

"I request you reside with us until they arrive. Go about the city as you please. However, the friend you spoke of was correct in warning you of the danger in certain sections. But be assured there are many fine people in San Francisco and beautiful and interesting places to see. We have grand theaters and some of the finest troupes of actors in the world come to put on plays."

"That friend I mentioned was named John Kelly. He was a violin player. Have you ever heard him perform?"

"Kelly. Yes, about six or seven years ago. He was a most skilled artist with his instrument. I would not forget him easily."

Tom was pleased at the reputation of the old fiddle player. One day he hoped to see him and tell him of that and to listen once again himself to the beautiful music.

"I accept your generous offer to stay here," said Tom. "I do have a little gold and can pay."

"Your gold has no value in this house," responded Ing. "I wish I could spend more time with you, for there are things of value we could tell each other. I especially would like to know more about your Oregon country. But Mingren and I have many hundreds of men to equip for a journey to the gold fields. If you should have returned here by evening, join us for conversation."

Ing and Mingren left. Tom lingered over another cup of tea and then went to his room. He slipped his six-gun under the belt of his trousers and buttoned his coat over it. The whole day was his and a large and unknown city beckoned for his exploration. Perhaps he might look for the blond woman who tried to shoot him with his own gun.

Tom walked hurriedly along the streets of Chinatown. Businesses of every description lined the avenues and thoroughfares. People crowded each other and peddlers came and went, balancing baskets of their wares on bending shoulder poles.

At a few of the business places and homes, there were men Tom thought were guards similar to those at Ing's. In pairs or singly, they sat or stood on the porches or balconies near the entrances. They were dressed similarly to the men who guarded Ing's establishment. Their black eyes alertly roamed over the passing people.

Tom watched two such men for a few minutes. They did not stray from their posts. He wondered why some establishments had the guards, but others did not.

Tom walked on, drawn down the sloping streets toward the docks. He stopped once and bought a map for two cents. He came to Market Street and saw a tiny steam train. He slowed and watched the conveyance pass, a miniaturized version of the locomotive that had pulled the train he had ridden from Winnemucca.

At a men's clothing store, he outfitted himself in a soft new cotton shirt and wool trousers and coat. He bought a hat. The used clothing he tossed in a trash box of the store. He considered buying new boots, but settled for just having a cobbler put new soles and heels on the ones he had. After all, the old boots were sprung in all the right places to be comfortable for a man who intended to walk miles about the city.

The odor of some strange food floated out to the sidewalk. Tom sniffed at the delightful aroma. He was in a section of the town with many restaurants, the signs proclaiming them English lunch rooms, French cabarets, German wirtschafts, Italian osterie and half a score of other nationalities. He would sample their fare over the next days.

A gaunt, scraggily clothed man stood on a corner with an open Bible in his hands. He was haranguing the pedestrians and men on the passing wagons about their sinful ways and saying that it was time to repent. He often broke his speech to quote the Bible without looking at it. No one paid him the slightest attention.

In front of the Grand Hotel, Tom encountered a woman on the sidewalk. She moved with a free swinging stride. She was dressed in a black bolero jacket and sweeping silk skirt. The woman looked at Tom with large gray eyes from behind the thinnest lace falling from the brim of her broad hat.

Tom stared at the attractive and handsomely dressed woman. She laughed lightly at his obvious admiration and passed on.

Tom smiled back as the woman swept by. The town held many beautiful women. Some of them were quite vicious and dangerous. And somehow that added to the appeal of this city on the ocean.

Tom recalled the woman and the men of the night attack. The

men were dead. What of the woman? What would he do if he found her?

He reached the wharves. The fog still held sway there, but it was thinning. The sun was a pale moon, striving to break through.

Tom saw a pier that had a schooner, two clipper ships and a steamship tied up to it. He walked out along the wooden platform. The hurry-skurry pace of loading and unloading had not diminished from the day before and he often had to step aside to avoid the workmen and the piles of ship freight.

A puffing steam crane was hoisting a cargo net full of long, narrow crates aboard one of the clipper ships. Curious as to what might be the contents of the containers, Tom drew near one of the seamen. "What is in those boxes?" Tom questioned.

The man turned to look at the cargo being swung into the hold of the ship. "There's coffins in those crates. Each one has a dead Chinaman in it, all ready for burial back in their country."

"Are many bodies sent back to China?"

"Every man that can afford the charge has his body returned home. The *Flying Cloud* has two hundred of them going back. That French ship, *Asia*, on the next pier over is carrying three hundred and twenty corpses. Those who are poorer have just their bones sent back to China. That's cheaper, since it doesn't take as much room. The *Pacific* took seven hundred sets of bones last week. It was in all the newspapers. That was the biggest number ever on one ship."

Tom thanked the seaman and returned to the shore. He heard loud shouting along The Embarcadero where a large throng of men had assembled.

"Goddamn heathen coolies," yelled a man. Other men took up the call, turning it into a chant.

Tom pushed through the gathering to the front. Hundreds of Chinese men were filing down the gangway of a large steamship and coming along the wharf.

The Chinamen, each carrying a small bundle and formed up in a line two men abreast, moved toward the shore. They closely watched the much larger white men shouting unfriendly names at them.

The foreigners looked well fed to Tom until he noted their bulk was accounted for by two, perhaps three sets of clothing worn one over the other.

At the shoreward end of the wharf and under a portable shelter, two American port officials sat at a table. A Chinese interpreter and a pair of policemen stood beside them.

The Chinamen were queued up in two lines in front of the table facing the port officials. They answered a short series of questions and then the policemen searched them.

"What are the lawmen looking for?" Tom asked a middle-aged man in workmen's clothing standing near him.

"Opium," answered the man shortly.

The man suddenly yelled out. "Send them all back to China. Bastards'll do work for pennies and an American can't find a job that pays enough to live on."

The man lifted a half brick he had hidden beside his leg. He cocked his arm to throw.

Tom shouldered him and the brick flew over the heads of the Chinamen, struck the wooden decking and bounced into the onlookers on the far side. A man cursed and shook his fist across the wharf.

The man who had thrown the brick twisted to look at Tom. "Say, fellow, you made me miss. Why'd you do that?"

"You could kill a man with something that hard," replied Tom.

"Then you did it on purpose. Why you damn Chinaman lover, I'll smash your face."

Tom did not want a fistfight with one of the angry congregation of white men. He unbuttoned his coat to expose the butt of his six-gun. "Unless you are good with a pistol, don't push your luck too far," Tom said in a flinty voice.

The man swallowed, his Adam's apple pumping up and down. "I was just funnin', you know." He slid away into the crowd.

Tom wound his way closer to the inspection area and listened to the questions and watched the rough hands of the lawmen check the bodies and clothing of the Chinamen.

The small, brown men answered the queries in the briefest of words. They remained stoic and unmoving to the prodding fingers. Yet Tom saw the doubt and uncertainty in their eyes. They were brave men to make such a dangerous journey. Many of them would die in the so-called Golden Hills.

Tom walked away from the docks. He had gone but a short distance when an uproar of angry shouts erupted. He glanced back. Two blocks from the inspection station and out from under the protective eyes of the policemen, white men were throwing mud and stones at a group of Chinamen.

A man, apparently a guide, perhaps one of Quan Ing's men, was gesturing and calling for the new arrivals to come more quickly after him. The men broke into a trot and drew away from the abusive and threatening Americans.

Tom left the docks. Following the whims that caught him, his route angled onto unknown avenues and streets. He talked with scores of people about what he saw.

In the evening, he gradually directed his footsteps toward the high part of the city on the sand hills.

On a crooked little street in the edge of Chinatown, he found a strange sign over a doorway. The words read: "Pipes and Lamps Always Convenient."

Tom stepped inside and peered about a small, smoke-stained room.

A fat Chinaman reclined in a wicker rocking chair that faced the door. Four cots covered with dirty blankets were behind him.

One of the beds was occupied by an old Chinese man. He lay with eyes half shut, like a dead man.

On the floor by his head a lump of dark substance the size of a hazel nut stewed and fried in a bowl over a lamp. A long pipe stem extended from the bowl to the old man's mouth. He sucked on it and opened his eyes to lazily watch the smoke curl up around the lamp. He drew on the stem again.

His eyes grew more glazed. His old face took on a haunting, faraway look. The pipestem fell from his slack lips.

Tom remembered the death of Yutang. Was this man lying on a dirty cot in San Francisco also sailing away home to distant China?

A second aged man slid sideways past Tom and entered. He paid the man in the wicker chair a quarter and received a small portion of opium and a pipe. He hurried to one of the cots and began to light the lamp.

"It costs a nickel to watch and a quarter to smoke," said the man in the chair. "You owe me a nickel at the least. Do you want a pipe?"

"No. Here is your nickel."

Tom wandered slowly up the hill streets. This day he had seen beautiful things and ugly things, selfish people, sad and frightened people. What did it all add up to? Where was the logic to it? He would ask Quan Ing about the meaning. Perhaps he would travel to Los Angeles and discuss them with John Kelly. Old men should have the answers and be able to tell him the many things he wanted and needed to know.

Tom hastened his steps. Tonight he would have supper with Quan Ing and Mingren, and tomorrow walk many more of the streets of this amazing town of San Francisco. He would check the docks daily until the ship *American Wanderer* sailed into port.

CHAPTER 18

Pak stood on the bow and stared ahead as the clipper ship *American Wanderer* came through the Golden Gate and into San Francisco Bay. A low, dark overcast hung over the water, restricting the range of his sight to a half mile or less. Mist stretched down like thin curtains from the clouds. Choppy waves ran before a fresh northwest wind.

The ship passed Alcatraz Island on the port side and swung to a southeast course. A patter of rain ran over the ship's deck and rattled on the oilskins of the deckhands hurrying to adjust sail to the new heading.

Pak went along the deck to the open hatchway of the wheelhouse. He desired to know more of how this sleek ship was handled. He stood unobtrusively, yet where he could see inside and hear.

The captain noticed Pak. He nodded at the silent Chinaman. The man had been all over the ship, watching every aspect of her operation. As an upper deck passenger, he had the run of the ship except the officers' and crew's quarters. He always kept himself out of the way of the working crew.

"Mr. Connel, we should be at the pier in San Francisco in an hour," the captain said to the first officer. "Let's hope the fog doesn't become worse."

"Yes, sir," responded Connel. "Do you want to use our own long boats for docking or the harbor charter boats?"

"Our seamen need the practice after all these weeks at sea. Use four of our boats. Seeing how the wind is coming, put two on the bow and two on the stern."

"Yes, sir. I'll make ready."

The long wooden piers of the city became visible bit by bit in the fog. The ship changed heading to take position for docking. Four of the six long boats were lowered by straining crewmen.

Sailors slid down into the bobbing boats. Ship's lines were tossed to them from the deck. The seamen in the boats bent to their oars and took the slack out of the lines.

The last sail dropped and was lashed down. The ship began to drift under the shove of the northwest wind. The captain called orders from the wheelhouse and Connel relayed them to the chief bos'n and his seamen in the boats on the water. The boats caught the ship, controlling the direction and speed of its movement. The vessel gently nudged the dock. The hawsers were made fast.

"Tell the chief a job well done," called down the captain.

"Yes, sir," answered Connel.

The captain continued to speak. "Inform the port authorities of our cargo and ask them to send representatives at the earliest opportunity. Tell Ziyang to prepare our live cargo for unloading. Move smartly, for there is not much daylight left."

"Yes, sir," replied the first officer.

"One last thing. The starboard watch can have twenty-four-hour shore liberty starting in one hour."

Connel saluted upward. "They will like that, sir."

Rain began to fall, fine misty droplets settling out of the dark heavens. The fog thickened.

Pak returned to the cabin and Lian. He said to her, "If it is agreeable with you, I would like to wait until the rain stops and let the men who have spent these many weeks in the foul hold of the ship leave first. I want to see how these Americans handle the arrival of so many of our people."

Pak did not tell Lian that he also wanted to lengthen the last few minutes with her as long as he could. In truth that was his most important reason.

"That is all right by me," said Lian. She stood close to Pak, very close, just barely not touching him. I am in no hurry, she thought.

She had been much dismayed upon being told by the elder Ho she was to be sent to a man in the land called America. She had said nothing, silently angry. The ordeal of going to a strange man had become even worse as she had grown to know the man Pak. More than that, she had developed a deep fondness for him. She knew he returned the affection.

The long journey was now over and new men would take

control over her. That safe feeling with Pak would be gone. She locked her hands together and steeled herself not to speak to Pak of her concerns.

They went outside the cabin and stood in the lee of its walls where the rain did not hit them. The first officer walked down the gangway and toward the city. He disappeared into the fog before reaching the end of the pier.

Part of the Chinese gold seekers were brought up from steerage and herded in a tightly packed mass on the upper deck. The men breathed deeply of the fresh air and smiled at each other with the pleasure of the voyage being ended. Then some of the smiles weakened as men surveyed the drizzling rain and the dismal mist obscuring their view beyond a hundred yards.

The first officer returned and came aboard the ship. He shouted orders at Ziyang and the seamen helping him with the steerage passengers.

The Chinamen began to file down the main gangway. The starboard watch of the crew left by the aft gangway and laughing and jostling each other playfully, proceeded along the wharf.

Tolman broke away from his shipmates and set off speedily toward Chinatown. He reached Pacific Street and turned left up it. He finally halted at a three-story house with a covered balcony extending out over the sidewalk.

Two men stood in the back of the balcony, blending almost completely into the murky shadows. When Tolman halted on the street and did not move, they came to the railing of the balcony and stared down at him.

"Why do you stop here? What do you want?" asked one of the men.

"I want to talk with Yaobang Hu. Tell him my name is Tolman."

"You wait right there," said the man. He turned and walked into the building. The second guard remained, staring through the gloom at Tolman.

The seaman was pleased with his plan. Hu was a high lieutenant in the Chee Kong Tong, the most secretive and violent in San Francisco. The members dealt in slave girls, protection and murder. Tolman had worked with them in times past and always at a goodly profit.

Never, however, had he made a profit and taken his revenge at the same time.

The first man came back and motioned for Tolman to climb the outside stairway. They searched him when he reached the balcony. One of the men took his navy revolver.

"I want my gun back," Tolman told the man.

"Maybe later. Go on in."

Tolman entered and looked nervously at the five Chinamen seated at the table. It was cool in the room; still he felt the sweat break out on the palms of his hands. Every one of these men was a killer and had no liking for any white man. They would murder him for the mere practice of doing it.

He settled his attention on a thin-faced man with part of his left ear missing. Yaobang Hu had risen up through the tong organization as a knife fighter. He showed the scars.

"Well, Tolman, I have not spoken with you in more than a year," said Hu in English. "Do you have something good for us from China?"

Tolman wondered how Hu knew the port of call of his last voyage. But then the tong leaders had spies in every major port and on most ships. Part of their strength was in knowing what occurred in business and politics.

"Something very valuable. A beautiful Chinese woman," said Tolman.

"Women are not very valuable. There are many of them. I could put out an order for a thousand and have them shipped from China on the next ship."

"Not like this one. She is special. She had a cabin above decks. A man came all the way across the ocean to bring her here."

"Almost all Chinese women are brought to America that way so they may arrive as virgins. Tell me why this one is so very rare and what you want from me."

"She is the most beautiful woman I have ever seen. She is not one you put in a crib or even in the fanciest whorehouse. She is the kind you sell to rich old men."

"We always have need for a woman such as that. How old is she?"

"Very young, sixteen, maybe seventeen."

"What do you want for this information?"

"Two hundred dollars."

Hu leaned forward. His lips curled in a wary smile and his eyes filled with mistrust. "That is cheap for the kind of woman you have told us about. There is more to this than what you say."

Tolman realized if he lied and Hu discovered it, his body would be found in the bay. "I want to see the man with her die."

"You want us to kill one of our countrymen for you?"

"Have your man give me back my pistol and I will go help you take the woman. The man will be with her. He can be disposed of then. We should hurry so we can catch them on the dock or at least on The Embarcadero. In the fog and rain, it should be easy to do."

"I agree," said Hu. He spoke to his men and then to Tolman. "These four will go with you. Let them do it silently. I do not want the noise of a gun. That would bring the Fearless Charlies. But you must go with them and point out the correct woman and man."

"Good. I want to be there when he is killed."

"Then it is arranged. Leave now. Tell the man to return your gun."

Hu pointed at one of his men. "That is Yun. He will pay you two hundred dollars when the woman is taken and if she is as you say."

Tolman nodded. He wondered if he should tell Hu what Ziyang had said, that the man with the woman was some kind of warrior. But then there should be no need for that, since Hu's men were expert killers themselves.

Pak and Lian watched the double line of Chinese men file slowly along the dock. The front end of the string of shuffling figures faded away into the fog while more men were still coming from the hold of the *American Wanderer*. A strange thought came to Lian. Was there really a city called Fahlanszeko, San Francisco, and a land of golden hills? Or were the men simply walking into nothing?

The rearmost of the gold seekers plodded into the mist and were gone. Pak did not stir. He would not be the first to end this final moment with Lian.

Ziyang came to them. "It is becoming late. Do you plan to leave the ship today?"

"Yes," replied Pak. "Please tell me how to get to Dupont Street."

Ziyang described the turns and the number of streets to cross on the route. He pointed at the weakening light on the wharf. "Dusk is here. But you still have time to reach your destination."

Lian and Pak entered the cabin. Lian lifted the two bundles that held all her possessions. Pak took up one small parcel.

"That is all you will bring?" asked Lian. "What of your other things?"

"This ship leaves on its return trip to Canton in four days. I have arranged for passage home on it."

Lian felt her heart shift within the cage of her chest. So soon she would be separated from him. When that happened, she would never see him again. She gripped the bundles tightly so she would not beg him to take her back with him.

"Shall we go?" asked Pak.

Lian merely nodded her head and did not look at him.

"Walk beside me instead of behind," Pak told Lian as they moved through the growing dimness on the pier.

The wind had grown still and the mist hung stationary. Beneath the wharf, wavelets struck the pilings with little wet slapping noises. All else was silent as if the fog had smothered any sound that might have come from the city.

The *American Wanderer* became lost in the vapors behind them and yet the shore could not be seen. Boxes, packing crates and heavy burlap sacks full of freight were piled here and there in mounds on the borders of the pier. Sufficient space had been left clear for two wagons to pass coming and going with loads. Tarpaulins were tied over the tops of the piles to keep the rain off.

Pak stopped abruptly. Ahead fifty feet or so two men had stepped from behind a stack of cargo. He saw them draw long bladed knives from inside their clothing.

Pak pivoted around to look for other danger. Two more men had come out into the center of the pier behind him to prevent his retreat. One held a knife, the other a hatchet.

He surveyed his opponents. They were all his countrymen. Why would they want to harm him? They should all be friends in this alien land.

The tong fighters began to close on Pak. He measured the lithe and sinuous menace of them.

A tingle touched Pak's spine. Next would come that wave of fear that all intelligent men have in a dangerous plight. Before that dark animal of fright could spring into full existence, Pak walled it off in a far deep recess of his mind. A man who must do battle can slay more enemies if he has conquered fear.

Pak swiftly planned his strategy for the killing that was soon to come.

The dark visages of the tong men evidenced no worry or nervousness, only a cool wariness as they approached the empty-handed Pak. They shifted their weapons to a more ready position.

Pak saw them evaluate Lian with a covetous eye. Then he understood the reason for the assault.

He pushed Lian back against a stack of goods. "Do not move from there," he ordered. "If they kill me, scream as loudly as you can and jump into the water. That may delay them so that if someone hears, they can come to your rescue before you are caught." He was sorry for the frightened expression on her face.

Pak jerked off his coat and tossed it aside. He coiled his queue on top of his head and bound it down tightly.

The tong fighters slowed, stiffening with suspicion as the man they thought most likely a farmer bound his hair in preparation for battle. The lone man reached to the back of his neck and a short, two-edged sword flashed into view.

One of the tong men laughed a brittle little laugh. "We have maybe cornered ourselves a tiger with a long tooth. But there are four of us and our blades are almost as long as his. Let us show him the points of our weapons."

The four men moved upon Pak. The ring closed to a radius of five strides. The man who had spoken had advanced more boldly than his cohorts and was a step nearer.

Pak knew he dared not let them come closer. For then, while he fought one, the others would rush upon his back and slay him.

He leaped at the nearest man. That person dodged aside and slashed out with his knife.

Pak cut off the outstretched arm at the wrist. With a reverse stroke, he severed the front of the man's neck. The mouth came open, howling soundlessly in death, and a great gout of blood spouted.

Pak whirled instantly. His arm with the sword was extended to its greatest reach. The three had charged in as Pak had known they would. The keen tip of his blade sliced the cloth covering a man's chest, and deeper, into the flesh, chipping off a flake of the white sternum bone to send it flying.

Without the slightest delay, the swing of the sword arced upward and then down. Pak had stepped in, shortening the distance to his adversary. Now the sword slashed through the top of his opponent's shoulder, and onward, cleaving the ribs to the waist.

A horrible expunging of air jetted out as the blade bit into the man's lungs. He retained his feet for a brief moment, an unbelieving expression on his visage. He toppled to the side.

Pak saw the courage of the tong fighters breaking. But he was too wise in the ways of war to let one foe escape to return and threaten him another day. He sprang at the man on the left.

The man stabbed out with his knife. He was slow and Pak easily struck the knife hand, severing the fingers. The knife fell to the deck of the pier. Pak took the man's head with a level cross swipe of the sword.

The tong man put out his stump of a hand as if seeking support from the air, then collapsed.

Pak looked at his last adversary. Fear was in the man's eyes, moving below the shiny black surface like water slugs. The man hurled his hatchet at Pak and tried to bolt past. The hatchet missed.

Pak lunged, meeting the man at right angles. He thrust the point of the sword out, plunging it deeply into the man's side.

The injured man screamed, a harrowing pitch. He swerved away from Pak and continued to run, blindly. He began to lean to the side and veer toward the water. The decking of the pier vanished from beneath his feet. Still screaming, he vanished into the bay.

Pak rotated around to check for other enemies. His body pulsed with the knowledge the battle was over and he was still alive. The stench of blood and the screams filled him with a wild frenzy for killing and the strength of twenty in his arms. He sucked in a breath of cold, moist air and trembled with the sweetness of it.

Tolman came out from behind a mound of cargo. He carried a navy revolver in his hand.

Pak noted the movement and turned to face it squarely. He let his breath out with an audible sigh. The battle was not yet over.

Tolman smiled. With the dead Chinamen on the dock, he could shoot this man and simply walk off. The law would think another Chinaboy had committed the murder. Tolman would take the woman to Hu himself.

Tolman called out to Pak. "You heathen bastard, I always believed in the back of my head that I'd have to kill you myself."

The seaman motioned at Pak with his hand. "Why don't you come over here and try that little sword on me? I'll show you how fast a bullet is."

Pak regarded the pistol. The man held it with a skillful familiarity. Never could Pak charge across the thirty feet separating them and kill the man. He would be shot down within the first two or three paces.

In the half darkness, he could leap into the bay and by swimming underwater have a good chance for survival. He discarded that thought, for never would he desert Lian to be taken prisoner.

The white man wanted him nearer; that was obvious from the hand signal. Well, that was the only way Pak could use his sword.

Pak stared at the man, trying to capture his eyes. However, the man looked past him and fastened on something there.

Pak turned. A tall American, quite young, stood a few feet behind him. His coat was unbuttoned and the tail shoved back. A pistol in a holster was buckled on his side.

Pak felt the black, cold fingers of death touch him. His enemy from the ship had a comrade. Never could Pak hope to slay both of them.

CHAPTER 19

The young American focused his attention on Lian. Pak saw him study her beautiful face and peer into her sloe eyes. Then the American's intense stare skipped to Pak. He said in Chinese, "Are you Pak Ho?"

"I am Pak Ho."

"Then move aside and let me handle this."

Pak moved from between the two foreigners. He stood prepared to rush and cut with his sword as the need arose.

Tom called out to Tolman. "The fight is over. This man won fairly. Let it drop and walk away alive."

Tolman licked his lips. The fellow had not touched his gun while he already held his. He eased the barrel up a few inches. Nothing had changed except that there were now two men to shoot. He jerked his gun up to fire.

Tom's hand plunged down and came up with his six-gun. His thumb cocked the weapon as it rose and his finger tightened on the trigger. He fired.

A bone-shattering blow slammed Tolman in the chest. His view of the men and the dock tilted as he fell. One last thought flashed in Tolman's mind—how could a man be so quick? He died before he hit the planking of the pier.

"The shots will be heard," Tom told Pak. "We must leave this place at once. There is always a policeman on the docks."

Tom grabbed up Lian's bundles, took her by the hand and hastened her away into the fog. He heard the thud of Pak's feet at his side.

Tom led the girl and man away from the docks of The Embarcadero and up the hills toward Chinatown. As they climbed, the darkness thickened and congealed about them. They passed a lamplighter moving from one gas streetlight to the next, reaching up with his flaming torch to touch them off.

They walked onward under the fog-shrouded light spills. Night strollers passed them, silhouettes without faces, who paid them no attention.

Pak slowed and felt for the opening of the scabbard and slid the weapon into place and out of sight on his back. He said to Tom, "How did you know we were on the pier?"

"Each evening, I came to The Embarcadero and asked the names of all the ships that had come into port during the day. A short time ago I met a group of seamen who told me they were off the *American Wanderer* and which pier it was tied up at. I came to meet you."

"It was very fortunate for us that you did. I owe you two lives."

"You owe me nothing. I was only repaying past favors done for me. Also, I promised to bring the woman safely to Oregon."

Dupont Street and Quan Ing's establishment were reached. Tom rapped on the side entrance with his knuckles.

"This is Tom Gallatin. Open, please," he called.

A small portal slid back and a man's face appeared. "Who is that with you?" asked the guard.

"Pak Ho and Lian Ah. They are expected by Quan Ing."

"All right," said the guard. He closed the portal and swung the door wide.

A second guard stood farther inside the room. Both had their sharp knives drawn.

The first man gestured for Tom and the others to come inside. He said, "Quan Ing has instructed me to tell you to see him at once. Something terrible has happened. He and several other men are in the store."

Tom guided the way along the hall. He heard men talking as he shoved open the door to the store.

Ing, Mingren, a man Tom did not know and four guards sat at a table. The unknown man sprang up as Tom entered.

He cried out, "Tom, they have killed Sigh and all the other men."

Tom felt the shock of what was said as he recognized Guofeng. It was nearly impossible to believe this ragged scarecrow of a man was the same person he had known in the Snake River Valley. His face had a haunted look, his eyes had a fever and were sunk deeply in their sockets.

Pak cursed. He moved up beside Tom. "I am Pak Ho, Sigh's cousin. Tell me what happened."

Guofeng rushed up to them. He caught Tom's arm. "The bandits came back, seven of them with rifles. I knew them. All except for two. They hid on the mountainside in the brush above Sigh's camp and shot them, every one.

"They chopped off Sigh's head with an ax and the heads of four others who were only wounded by the rifles. Every person was thrown in the river."

Guofeng clutched Tom's arm more fiercely. "You should have killed the bandits when you had the chance. Yutang has been proved correct in an awful way."

Guofeng turned around slowly to look into every man's face in the room. "The foreign devils killed thirty-one of our people, our friends and relatives. I have followed them over many hundreds of miles and for so many days that I have forgotten the number.

"The murderers were riding horses and I was only walking so I was far behind and lost track of them. But as I lay hidden and watched them slay Sigh and his friends, I heard them say the name of this city, San Francisco. So I went to Winnemucca where I could catch a train. There I questioned some of our people. One man told me a group of white men caught the train heading west. I believe they came here to San Francisco. They should have arrived four days ago."

Guofeng went to his chair and sat down. "Honorable Ing, they must be punished for the horrible thing they did. Tom, you can go among the white men and search. Find them and use your pistol as you did that day on the Snake River."

"San Francisco is a very large city," said Ing. "Hundreds of white men come and go each day. It will be difficult to locate them, but it can be done.

"Mingren, go tell our people what has happened and that we need their help. Go even to the other tong societies. In most things they are against us. In this effort they will assist. Tell everyone to listen and watch and find those men who have come from the Oregon country in the last four days."

"Would it not be wise to post a reward for information?" asked Mingren.

"Yes. But do not post it as we do other notices. Say it quietly in people's ears. The city officials must not hear of this. We must seek our own justice. Make the reward one thousand dollars in gold. That is enough to cause a man to tell us what he knows."

"The bandit leader holds his head back and twisted to the side," said Guofeng. "Yutang must have done that to him."

"I will tell this to the people," Mingren said. "I go now to spread the word. It is dark and not much can be done tonight. The search can start fully at daylight."

"I have walked the streets of this town for several days," said Tom. "I know it better than most people and I know the kind of men these outlaws are. They will stay in only one part of town, on The Embarcadero or the Barbary Coast. I am not going to wait until tomorrow. This night is just beginning. I will start to hunt for them now."

Ing nodded in agreement. "This is the best time of day to see them walking about. Mingren, go do as we have discussed. First though, send our off-duty guards to me. I will send them out onto the streets to ask questions and help Tom to search."

"At once," said Mingren. He bowed and left.

Pak spoke to Tom. "I too shall seek the killers of my Cousin Sigh. Since I do not know my way about the avenues of this city, may I walk with you? You question the white men for information. I can ask the men of my race. Each of us shall get truer answers that way."

"That is a good idea," Tom said.

Ing spoke to Pak. "We have not yet been introduced. I am Quan Ing. You have arrived in San Francisco at a bad time. However, I welcome you to my home."

Pak bowed. "Thank you. Even in faraway Canton, I have heard of your hospitality."

Ing turned to Lian. "And you also are welcome, Lian. The women of my family will be pleased to have your company."

Lian bowed. "You are most generous."

"We should go," Tom said to Pak.

"I am ready."

"Do you want a weapon?" Ing asked Pak.

"I have a sharp blade," replied Pak.

"I can certainly vouch for that," said Tom.

Pak and Tom went from the store onto the street.

The singsong chanting of the Chinese crib girls rang eerily along the dark, foggy block with many doorways. Men slowed to look through the latticework of the windows and talk with the women. A man consented to the price and entered one of the narrow portals.

Tom and Pak stood at the end of the square. They had searched down Market Street, making detours into the Barbary Coast on Pacific, Kearny and Broadway Streets. Every saloon, gambling hall, hotel and bordello they encountered had been entered, and to the extent possible, examined for the presence of one or more of the outlaws. Questions had been asked. All the answers had been in the negative.

Several hours had passed since they had left Quan Ing's and now they were at the end of Market Street near The Embarcadero.

"What kind of place is this?" asked Pak, indicating the numerous doorways opening onto the sidewalk.

"The women are whores," responded Tom. "Each has a little room of her own."

"Yes. I understand. They are *chinoises,* daughters of joy."

"Many men come here," said Tom. "The bastards we look for could also have visited. One of these women may remember seeing the crooked-neck man and have some information about him. You begin asking questions here and I'll go to the opposite end and work back to meet you."

"Good, let us hurry."

Tom and Pak discovered no woman recalling the men that were sought.

They walked west on Market Street, checking the faces of the male pedestrians they met.

Both men heard the patter of slippered feet as a man came out of an alleyway and fell in behind them. When the steps increased in tempo and drew nearer, Pak and Tom whirled to face the unknown person.

The man stopped abruptly. He flinched back and raised his arm protectively as the two men bore down on him.

"Wait! Wait!" he exclaimed in Chinese. "I mean you no harm."

"Then why do you follow and hurry close to our backs?" questioned Pak.

"I have heard a Canton man and a white man together would be on Market Street, or perhaps the Barbary Coast, looking for men from Oregon, one of them a crooked-neck man." He lowered his arm. He was old, yet still looked strong.

"We are those men and you speak correctly," said Pak. "Do you have news of such a man?"

"There is a reward? I have also heard that whisper."

"One thousand American dollars in gold if we locate them all."

The man chuckled gleefully. "Then give me the gold, for I can tell you where to find them."

"We must see them first and then you get paid," replied Pak.

"How do I know you won't cheat me?"

"Do you know Quan Ing? He is the person to pay the reward. I am Pak Ho and I also add my promise."

"I know Quan Ing. He is an honorable man and lives by his word." The man looked craftily around. "My name is Tan Ying. Remember that. I work on the docks loading the big ocean ships. New guards were hired to patrol the pier opposite Shipley Street and protect the warehouse there. They are men from Oregon and one has a crooked neck. He is mean and hates Chinese people. Remember, I alone have shown you the path to the men."

"Enough talk," said Pak. "Show us the place."

"Come," said Ying.

The rolling fog was thick on The Embarcadero. The flare from the streetlamps helped but little to light the way. Tan Ying walked hurriedly, moving through familiar territory.

He led them to a giant warehouse, one among many lining The Embarcadero, and to a door in its side. "In there," whispered Ying. "They are in there."

"Be quiet and listen for a moment," said Tom.

On the seaward side of The Embarcadero, a ship creaked as it wallowed at its moorage. The waves could be heard pounding the pilings of the piers. All was quiet in the warehouse.

"How many entrances to the building?" Pak asked Ying.

"Four. One on each end wide enough for the largest wagons to pass through. There is another door the size of this one on the opposite side from us. This is the place the guards enter and leave. All but this one are secured by very strong padlocks. Only the owner has a key to open them. The guards lock this door on the inside."

"Where do the guards stay when they are on duty and not patrolling the pier?" asked Tom.

"Come, you can see for yourself," said Ying. "There is a broken board where a wagon hit the wall and you can see inside." Ying guided them to a splintered hole in the side of the warehouse.

"Look through here," said Ying.

Tom and Pak stooped and peered inside. A lamp on a table cast a yellow stain on the dark cave of the warehouse. Six men sat around the table playing cards.

"Luck is with us," said Tom. "They are the ones. I recall four of them from that day on the Snake River. The leader of the gang is not there."

"Let me look," said Ying. He squatted to peer inside. "Only two of the men are on guard duty at any one time. The others come and go, but often gather here to play cards. The one you described sometimes goes to that big saloon on The Embarcadero to drink and gamble."

"These men are trapped within the building. They can be killed now and then we find the last one," said Pak.

"How do we get in with all the doors locked?" Tom asked.

"You mean how do I get in," said Pak. "The dead men were my countrymen." His voice became edged. "One was my cousin. I must be the one to take revenge."

Tom stepped close to better see Pak. "There are six men with guns in there. We both must do the job."

"We would only get in each other's way. Further, you need light to shoot and that would make a lot of noise. Everyone would know your location. I will knock out the lamp and fight them in the dark. My sword will be better than your gun."

Tom's face was hard as he evaluated Pak's position. He wanted to be part of the attack.

"I will not allow you to go inside with me," Pak said. "You would be a hindrance."

Tom gauged the unblinking stare of the Chinaman. He would

have to fight the little man to make him change. Tom could not do that.

"Then go kill them, my Chinese friend," said Tom.

"We must discover a way for me to get inside," Pak said.

"I can help you," said Ying. "The children sometimes come to the docks and play tricks on the guards of the warehouses. They run around the buildings and hit on the walls with sticks and rocks. It is all a game with the little ones. The guards do not like it. But one always comes outside and chases the children away. The door is unlocked during the short period the guard is doing that."

"Can you make the same racket?" Pak asked.

"It is nothing special. I will show you." Ying hunted about on the ground until he found a stone of a size that suited him. "Get ready," he said.

Tom and Pak moved into the shadow of the nearby warehouse. The Chinaman began to bind up his hair on the top of his head.

Ying ran along the side of the warehouse, striking its wall with the rock and yelling in a high-pitched, childish voice. He circled the building and came back past the door. A tall man flung it open and raced after the smaller figure of Ying.

Pak stared at the gaping black hole of the door as he finished binding up his hair. He felt the tingle and slither of his anger and hate like a great snake uncoiling in his stomach.

He said to Tom, "Tonight I might die. But before I do, I will inflict terrible punishment upon those murderers. Guard the door. If I am not the one to come through the door, kill that man for me."

"It would be a pleasure," Tom said.

Pak dashed for the opening. Tom saw the cold, polished steel of his sword wink as it caught a ray from the nearest streetlight. Then Pak melted into the gloom of the warehouse, a lone warrior to fight six men in the vast blackness. If Pak could put out the light without getting shot.

The guard returned empty-handed and entered the warehouse. Tom heard the door being barred from within. He crept to the broken board in the wall and knelt.

Ying came up beside him and spoke in a whisper. "It went just as I said."

The guard reseated himself and picked up his cards. "How many of you looked at my cards?" he asked.

"Nobody touched them," said a man testily. "The bet is a quarter to you. Call, raise or fold."

Tom saw Pak's dark figure rushing toward the card players. His arm was outstretched. The extended sword slashed the lamp from the table. Glass crashed and complete darkness engulfed the cave of the warehouse.

A volley of gunshots reverberated from the walls of the building. The pitiless battle had begun.

CHAPTER 20

Tom moved to the door and pulled his six-gun. He waited, his ear tuned to the smallest noise, and watched intently for motion in the fog among the warehouses or on The Embarcadero. The shots had been substantially deadened by the enclosed walls of the building, but still a policeman might have heard the gunfire and come to investigate.

From inside the warehouse, a shrill cry broke the silence, to be abruptly cut off. A few minutes later there was a commotion of falling crates.

In the next hour, Tom heard three pistol shots. Each was from a different part of the warehouse. The second hour was entirely silent.

Tom wondered who was yet alive. Had Pak crept up on the white men one after the other and slain them with his sword? Or had one of the pistol slugs torn a hole in him and he lay dead? And were the white men uncertain of their foes' whereabouts and afraid to make a light?

Tom stiffened as a slight noise came from behind the door and someone whispered. He began to back away from the building.

The door was flung open and a man charged out. He held a pistol in his hand. A second man sprang through the opening.

The first man saw Tom outlined in the fog by the distant street-light. He snapped a shot at him.

Tom heard the zip of the bullet past his cheek. He lifted his gun and fired at the outlaw.

As the man fell, the second jerked up his pistol. Before he could trigger the gun, Tom killed him.

Hurriedly Tom ran to the side entrance. Pak must be told that two men had come outside. Tom jumped through the black hole of the open door, sprang sideways and hunched low.

"Pak, two men are dead outside," Tom called into the murky depths of the warehouse.

"Good," said Pak not twenty feet away.

Tom was startled by the nearness of the man. If he had hesitated to call out, Pak could have unknowingly cut him to death with his sword.

Pak spoke again. "I heard them whispering and moving, but I was too slow to overtake them before they found the door."

"I stopped them," said Tom.

"Tom, I am hurt and will need some help to get out of here."

"Talk to me so I can find you."

"Come this way. We must hurry and leave this place."

"Got you," said Tom. He put one of Pak's arms over his shoulder and, half carrying him, left the building.

"Let us go to a light so I can see your wound," said Tom. He continued toward the nearest streetlight. Ying came out of hiding and tagged along.

"My luck was bad and one of the bullets struck me when I knocked out the light," Pak said. He was silent for a few steps. "There is still one more of the killers. We must go and find him."

"You are not in condition for more fighting," Tom replied.

Pak laughed a faint chuckle. "Correct. But you are strong and brave. I would hire you as a Triad Warrior. I leave the last bandit to you."

They halted under the light and Tom opened Pak's coat and blouse. A bullet had torn through the flesh of his waist. Blood welled freely from both the entry and exit wound.

"The gunshot by itself is not all that bad," said Tom. "But you have lost much blood. Your pants are soaked with it. That's why you are weak. The bleeding must be stopped or you will die."

"There is a doctor not more than six or seven blocks from here," Ying said.

"Then we will take Pak there," said Tom.

"Ying can help me to walk that distance. You go and finish our task."

"The saloon where the crooked-neck man drinks and plays cards is the Seamen's Joy on The Embarcadero, just south of Market Street," Ying told Tom.

"Where's the doctor's office?" Tom asked.

"On Fremont, near Minna. His name is Traverson. He has treated many gunshot wounds and is very good," said Ying.

"I will be there later," Tom told Pak.

Tom entered the Seamen's Joy Saloon. He slowed and blinked at the strangely brilliant white gas flames in the lamps that illuminated the interior.

The saloon was outstandingly spacious, being quite wide and open upward for the height of two stories. Tom estimated there were two hundred people in the building. Men stood shoulder to shoulder at the long bar stretching away on his right the full length of the room. Beyond a chest-high wooden partition were twenty-five gambling tables, all chairs occupied and men standing, waiting for a seat at the game of chance. Twenty couples on the dance floor swung to wild and loud music. Several women, all of them clothed in short, brightly patterned Chinese silk dresses, served drinks or talked with the male patrons.

Tom removed his coat and draped it over his left arm. He walked along the bar looking at the reflections of the men's faces in the mirror on the back wall.

At the edge of the dance floor he stood and waited until all the dancers had circled, promenading past him. One of the girls noticed the scrutiny of the tense young man and winked at him.

Tom did not respond to the girl's flirtation. He walked to the partition of the gambling area. Methodically he began to run his sight over the men at every table. The standing people blocked his view of some of the seated players. He changed positions so he could see every face and not miss his quarry.

At one of the tables in the far back sat a man with his head canted upward a little and twisted to the right. His back was turned, but still Tom sensed something familiar about him.

He laid his coat on the partition and checked his six-gun in its holster. When Guofeng had first described the deaths of Sigh and the others on the Snake, Tom had held his grief and anger under control. Now as he went toward the man that might be the leader of the killers, all his hate burst out.

For a fragment of time, Tom was glad he was going to kill a man. His father had told him not to get to like killing. Did that apply when a man deserved to die?

Five players and the dealer were at the table. The pot had been opened and the initial round of wagers made.

"Cards?" said the dealer.

The players called the number they wanted. The dealer flipped the red pasteboards from the deck and sent them spinning to each man.

Tom had wound around through the crowd. Now he could see the face of the man he had spotted across the room. Tom's lips drew back and his teeth showed cruelly white as he recognized the outlaw chief. He felt joyous in a ferocious sort of way, anticipating the coming battle. He pushed two men aside and came near the players.

"I bet three hundred dollars," said a man in a naval officer's uniform.

The next three players folded their cards and dropped out of the game. It was Keggler's turn. He riffled his cards and eyed the mound of paper and gold currency on the table.

He counted his money lying on the table. "I call and raise you three hundred dollars." He shoved all his money into the pot and grinned at the naval man.

"I'm dropping out," said the dealer.

The naval officer placed gold coins in the center of the table, hesitated and then added some more. "I call and raise you again by one thousand dollars."

Keggler scowled as he checked his cards. Then he smiled. "I guess I'll have to go into the bank."

He unbuttoned the front of his shirt. His hand fumbled there a few seconds and then came out with a golden cube covering most of his palm.

A wave of astonished voices came from the players and onlookers. "God, ain't that beautiful," someone said in a worshipping tone.

"I cover your bet with one thousand dollars in this," said Keggler and laid the heavy cube of gold on the pile of money already on the table.

"No damn bet!" Tom said in a savage voice.

All eyes in the vicinity jumped to fix on Tom. A shocked expression swept over Keggler's countenance.

Tom shouted in a strident voice. "This man killed thirty-one of my friends in Oregon for that gold. He cut off their heads with an ax."

"You are a goddamned liar," hissed Keggler. He sprang erect, his dark eyes furious and squinted almost shut. "I should have killed you long ago."

"Do it now, you murdering sonofabitch."

Keggler's hand dipped for his pistol.

Tom drew, never more swiftly. The six-gun bucked in his hand. A damn pleasant feeling.

A sudden wind seemed to whip Keggler's shirtfront and he was slammed backward to the floor. He lay there a moment, then struggled to his knees and stared at Tom. "Damn you to hell," he said in a voice hoarse and ghastly, like a raven's croak. He began to lift his pistol.

Tom said, "You go there first and wait for me. Wait a very long time." He fired a second shot beside the first in the outlaw's chest.

Tom stepped to the table and picked up the golden cube. He raised his hands aloft—the gold in one hand, his six-gun in the other.

"I take this gold to give to the families of my dead friends." Tom's voice cut through the silence of the crowded room like a sharp blade. "If any man here disagrees with that, then let him come forward." He pivoted slowly, his challenging eyes boring out of his hard, young face.

No man moved in the saloon. Tom left.

Tom leaned on the pilings at the end of the pier and stared seaward. The clipper ship *American Wanderer* had caught the wind and was racing for the Golden Gate and the open sea. Though miles away, the ship's tall masts and the great sails could be seen plainly, a narrow pyramid of white against the blue of ocean and sky.

Tom felt a loneliness creeping in. Pak and Lian were homeward bound to Canton and the Pearl River Valley. A happy pair, from Tom's observations. They carried with them the golden cube. Pak would sell it and divide the returns among the families of the dead men who had found it.

Guofeng had left on his return journey to the valley of the

Snake River and his men there. Tom hoped his gold discovery at Triangle Mountain was very rich.

A gull cried out nearby as it skimmed in searching for bits of sea life with its quick, thin beak. The bird found a morsel and angled up, its wings scooping the wind, pressing it down to climb the soft ladder of air.

Tom turned away from the bird and the ocean and looked out over the docks and up at San Francisco, the city of beautiful white houses on the sand hills. It was a rich town. He would stay here, find a job. A man could become wealthy in this place, if he was strong and quick.

EPILOGUE

The Highbinders is fiction; however, it is based upon a true incident of a cold-blooded massacre of thirty-one Chinese miners on the Snake River near the mouth of Deep Creek in northeast Oregon.

J. K. Vincent, United States Commissioner, investigated the case. He wrote the Chinese Consul at San Francisco as follows about the wholesale butchery:

> ". . . was the most cold-blooded, cowardly treachery I have ever heard tell of on this coast, and I am a '49er; every victim was shot, cut up and stripped and thrown in the river."

Bodies of the miners were found at intervals for some months in the Snake River, as far as Panawawa, one hundred and sixty miles downstream.

The Imperial Chinese Government, through the Chinese Minister, Chang Yen Hoon, lodged a stiff complaint with the United States. The Minister stated:

> ". . . as the character of this case, wherein 31 lives were murdered and their bodies mutilated in a most shocking manner and thrown away, differs greatly from a common case of homicide. It is feared other wicked persons may, from their hatred of the Chinese, follow the examples of the murderers if not arrested and punished, which will affect the interest and safety of the Chinese residents there and elsewhere in the United States."

The United States paid $276,610 as indemnities, stating the payment was made ". . . out of humane consideration and with no reference to the question of liability for loss of Chinese life in the Northwest."

Though each member of the gang became known, not one was ever brought to justice. All eluded the law and escaped to other states.

The leader of the gang was killed during an argument in a card game in San Francisco.